the goalie and santa's little helper

A Holiday Romance

Final Score Series
Book Four

ginger scott

The Goalie & Santa's Little Helper

by USA TODAY bestselling author
GINGER SCOTT

Text copyright © 2024 Ginger Scott
(Little Miss Write, LLC)

No part of this book may be reproduced in any form or by any electronic or mechanical means, including information storage and retrieval systems, without permission in writing from the author. The only exception is by a reviewer, who may quote short excerpts in a review.

Without in any way limiting the author's exclusive rights under copyright, any use of this publication to "train" generative artificial intelligence (AI) technologies to generate text is expressly prohibited. The author reserves all rights to license uses of this work for generative AI training and development of machine learning language models.

This book is a work of fiction. Names, characters, places and incidents either are products of the author's imagination or are used fictitiously. Any resemblance to actual persons, living or dead, or events is entirely coincidental.

Ginger Scott

Cover design and formatting by Ginger Scott

Cover illustrations by Katy Mendoza

note from ginger

I hope you enjoy this sexy little winter trip back into the Final Score Series. If you haven't read the Final Score books yet, you can find them in Kindle Unlimited or print at all print book retailers.

Wishing you all an amazing holiday season. Now, turn up the spice.

;-)

Ginger

For you.

1 /
noah drake

NO MATTER how old I am, coming home and sleeping in my childhood bedroom instantly makes me feel like I'm ten again. It's a good feeling. A safe feeling. And if I close my eyes and lay back on the quilt my mom made from my old jerseys, I can almost convince myself I'm still that kid, the one whose entire world is wide open and possible.

Not that I don't love the path I'm on. Hockey is everything to me. It's the thread that's held the important people in my life together, tethering us through wins and losses, lessons and failures, comraderies and rivalries.

It's how I met my best friend when I was the new kid in town. I saw Anthony Bardot playing street hockey out in front of his house with his dad, and they invited me to give it a try. It turns out I was good. Better than Anthony, but I would never say that to him, at least not sober.

Anthony is how I met Francesca—*Frankie*. His sister. A pain in our ass from day one. Less a pain in *my* ass when she turned fifteen and started high school. And by the time she was eighteen and ready to head off to college last summer? I was more annoyed when Anthony was around. Those tables totally turned.

The soft knock at my door stirs me from my daydream, and I prop myself up on my elbows as my mom pushes the door open a notch.

"I wasn't sure if you were napping." Her lips tug up on one side, that sweet-yet-judgmental little smirk she gives when she's needling me about bad habits. I love a good nap. Always have. Some might call my naps actual sleeps, however, given the fact they usually last a good three hours.

"I got home ten minutes ago, Ma. I'm wide awake." It takes massive willpower to hold in my yawn. I give in after a few seconds when my mom's wry smile stretches into her cheek.

"Fine; I'm a little tired." My mouth contorts as I moan my way through the rest of the yawn.

I swing my legs around and plop my feet on the floor, forcing myself to sit up. The first step to staying awake is getting my ass off this bed. My mom steps into my room and takes a seat beside me, lifting my arm up dropping it over her shoulder. She thinks she needs to trick me into hugging her, but the truth is, I like it.

"Did you tell Anthony to bring Frankie over for dinner tonight?" I flinch when my mom mentions her name, but I don't think she notices. I haven't seen Frankie since the summer—when I crossed that line I swore to myself—and her brother—I'd never cross.

"I don't think she's home yet." I clear my throat as I

stand, slipping my feet into my Birkenstocks before busying myself with the massive suitcase I stuffed with dirty laundry.

"She got home yesterday. Her finals were done a day early and she wanted to get a jump on setting up at the ice rink."

Of course that's the first thing Frankie did. She's been playing Santa's helper at the local rink since junior high. Her dad, Coach Bardot, plays Santa, and the local paper lends out their photographer for the season to help raise money for the community center's holiday meal. Families drive hours sometimes just to lace up their skates on our outdoor rink and snap a pic with St. Nick when they're done. And every ten bucks donated goes right back to the people in our community who need it most. I used to tease her about playing an elf, taunting her that her skin was turning green. But damn, if it isn't one of the things I like about her most. In a selfish world, Frankie Bardot is anything but.

My mom's hip bumps into mine, scooting me over so she can take over unloading my wadded-up sweatshirts and twisted jeans.

"I know they have washers and dryers at Tiff University," she teases.

"Yeah, but my clothes smell so much better when you wash them."

"*Hmm*, that's because you don't wash them. This suitcase?" She flips it shut and flattens her palm on top, half of my dirty clothes still sandwiched inside. "It stinks,

Noah. Take the whole damn thing downstairs and shovel it in the wash."

She props one hand on her hip as she leans her weight on my suitcase and levels me with a hard stare.

"Fine," I huff playfully, tugging the suitcase toward me. I scurry out of her reach when I catch her rolling up one of my sweatshirts in my periphery. She swats at me and the sleeve grazes my thigh as I high step my way out of my room, my half-filled suitcase in my arms as I hoot with laughter on my way down the hallway.

"And find out if both Bardots are coming over for dinner tonight, would you?" she calls after me.

"Yes, ma'am," I holler back.

The adrenaline rush is immediate. I didn't exactly think I'd make it the entire winter break without seeing Frankie, but on my first day home? I was hoping to ease into a confrontation. I need more time to practice my words and perfect my excuses—not that an entire semester of radio silence wasn't enough time. I kept putting it off because that's what I do with hard things; I avoid them.

I flip open the top of the washer and push away the memory of Frankie's plump bottom lip as I shovel the last dregs of dirty socks and wrinkled T-shirts into the bin. Like a sign from the universe, though, my old high school hockey hoodie is the last piece of clothing I grasp—the same one I gave Frankie when I walked her home from the summer bonfire four months ago. My thumb runs over the embroidered letters of my last name as I let my head rest against the dryer door and summon the feel of her cheek against the pad of my thumb instead. She wore this sweatshirt home that night after I kissed her in the middle of the street between our two houses. I wanted her to keep it. Instead, she threw it at me a week later from the passenger window of her dad's truck as he drove her to the airport for her freshman year at Harbor State.

My phone buzzes in my pocket so I let go of the sweatshirt—*and the memory*—to close the washer door and start the cycle. I check the message alert as I head from the mudroom into the garage and feel around in the dark for the garage door opener. I barely register that it's a nearly nude pic from one of the Tiff puck bunnies. I press the button and shuffle toward the rolling door as I scratch at the back of my neck and stare at my phone screen. Getting pics like these used to shock me. Now? My message apps are filled with them. I don't even think half of them are real people, but rather AI bots trying to scam me into being their hockey-playing sugar daddy. The attention really ramped up this year, thanks to the rumors that I may be heading to Calgary.

I need to text Anthony about dinner, but before I can swipe my screen away from the image of the blonde stranger wearing a cropped hockey jersey—the hem only low enough to cover half of each nipple—I'm blocked by a massive garment duffel being shoved into my chest.

"What the—" My phone tumbles from my hand as my gaze lands on Frankie.

"My dad says you volunteered to play Santa. So here you go. Don't fuck it up." Frankie's eyes roll to the side and then down as she turns to march back across the street, but we both glance down at the same time, gazes locked on my very X-rated phone screen.

"Fuck," I mouth to myself, squeezing my eyes shut for a beat as if, somehow, I have the power to freeze time. Newsflash—I don't.

My eyes jet back to Frankie, just in time to catch her pursed lips pull in tight as a snarky little laugh puffs out her nostrils.

I stare at her back for a few seconds, cursing my shitty luck. Her wavy brown hair sways from shoulder to shoulder as she treks into the roadway, a deep red sweatshirt hiding the curves of her hips and ass in her black leggings.

"Frankie, wait!"

She spins around faster than I expected, and naturally, my words are nowhere near ready. I hold up a finger as I swing the garment bag over my right arm and squat to pick up my phone. I stammer out, "Hold on!" as I shuffle down the driveway. Frankie makes zero effort to meet me halfway.

That's fair.

I halt two or three steps from her and quirk a brow.

"Why am I Santa?" My chest squeezes, and my inner me kicks at my ribs for being a dumbass and leading with Santa. *Four months of rehearsals and that's what I say.*

Frankie pushes her tongue against the inside of her cheek, squinting the eye on the same side as she studies me for a tick.

"You need community service hours to graduate, remember?"

I swallow and croak out a soft, "Oh, yeah."

I do not remember.

Her eyes narrow. She's always been able to read my bullshit. It's why I never liked playing Uno with her when we were kids. I swear, she could tell what color I had left in my hand simply by studying my expression.

"You are kidding me!" She exhales a grumble as she pops a hand on one hip and glances toward her house over her shoulder.

"I kind of remember, sure." *Again. I do not.*

Her gaze snaps back to mine, and what looks like ache flashes across her eyes.

"You called my dad two weeks ago and begged him to let you wear the suit. You said your internship instructor would allow it to count for community service hours. Because of hockey. And because you're *oh-so-special*."

My mouth hangs open a hint as she makes finger quotes around a few keywords. Her words do ring a bell, and I'm pretty sure I made that call after a long afternoon drinking cold ones with the guys at Patty's. I'd just gotten back from my quick trip home for Thanksgiving. Frankie had opted to go to a friend's house near her school instead. A *guy* friend. Her brother was keen on emphasizing that part to me. At the time, concocting this elaborate scheme for forced proximity seemed the natural way to go. Faced with the reality of it now, though? What was I thinking?

"You know what? I'll just find something else to do this break. I know you love working with your dad for this, so tell him thanks, but—" I start to unload the garment bag back into her arms when she holds out a stiff open palm.

"He's in Palm Beach for ten days. Playing golf." Her mouth is a hard, flat line.

My mouth forms an "oh" despite the word getting stuck in my throat.

"Yeah. Apparently, he's always wanted to join his old college buddies for this trip, and he knew I would be in *good hands.*"

"You keep doing that air quote thing. I'm starting to think you're being sarcastic." I, of course, am being sarcastic. Frankie? She's just pissed.

"Like I said, Noah. You're wearing the red suit. Don't fuck it up." Her eyes glaze over, an almost emotionless expression drawing her mouth down as she turns her back to me again and finishes her trip back to her house.

I get about five seconds alone to scold myself before her brother steps out their front door and jogs over to my side of the street. He points a thumb over his shoulder.

"What's this I hear about you playing Santa?" He eyes me skeptically. I've never known for certain whether he saw me kiss his sister that night. But the conversation we had the morning after when he told me Frankie was thinking about dropping her scholarship to Harbor to follow us to Tiff, sure felt oddly timed. It was the way he added that little bit, asking if I had any idea why she would suddenly be considering that. The squint in his eyes was much like it is now.

Accusatory.

Pointed.

Threatening.

"Shit, man. I mentioned to your dad that I needed community service hours for graduation, and I guess he came up with this." I glance around, doing my best to look put off by the entire thing.

"Oh, wow. That sucks, dude. And my dad's out of town, so you get *all* the shifts. Ha! I guess I could split it with you. How many hours do you need?"

I swallow down the lies piling up and squint as I glare at the horizon. If Anthony ever finds out I don't need any hours, that I made the whole damn thing up, he's going to knock my teeth in.

"Forty, I think? Maybe more. I'm not sure. I've gotta look." Forty seems like a lot. But it also doesn't seem like enough time for me to make things right with Frankie.

"Damn, okay. We can still skate in the mornings. And when my dad gets back in town, I know he'll want to spend time with you on the ice." Anthony pats an open palm against my chest, and I manage to remember the entire reason I was coming to see him in the first place.

"Hey, you coming over for dinner?" I tilt my head toward my house.

"Your mom's meatballs? Uh, yeah."

The two of us trudge up my driveway together, his sister's invitation quickly lost under the mountain of bullshit and lies. *Ho, ho, ho.*

2 /
frankie bardot

I'M A GRINCH. I've never been one before, but this year? My holiday spirit is in the toilet.

It was enough to hype myself up to face Noah over break, knowing he and my brother would be inseparable. I planned on using my dad as the buffer. He'd shuffle the boys off to the arena to get their morning skating in and maybe some side work, then come back in the afternoon to hang out with me at the North Pole. But just as he always does, Noah Drake came along and screwed it all up —made it about him. As if my life hasn't already been enough about him.

Even my North Pole looks more like an alleyway right now. This set is only a few years old, but the backdrop is dingy and faded. I guess when the storage area is a metal shed tucked in the corner of our yard, I shouldn't expect much.

"Do you want to build everything first? Or paint first?" My best friend Mazy raises both fists, one clutching a roller, the other a hammer. My shoulders drop with my sigh, and I reach for the hammer.

"I guess it's easier to paint standing up, so grab the nails."

I bend down, grab the cutout toy factory by the roofline, and lift it in place. My high school theater friends and I built this set three years ago using some of the leftover pieces from our winter production that year. It's not the most professional-looking backdrop, but it makes for some pretty photos when the colors are bright, and the lights are strung. Besides, kids are happy if you put a cheery Santa in the middle of just about anything. Well, except for the ones who are terrified. My dad is always good at easing fears. This season, though? I can't say I'll blame any of them for running away from the new Santa. *Imposter.*

Mazy hands me a few nails that I hold between my lips. She lifts the adjoining wall, and I shift the wooden brace in place while balancing the hammer and reaching toward my mouth for a nail.

"You need a hand?"

Noah's voice seems to come out of nowhere, and I nearly swallow the remaining nails. I drop the brace, and it slides down the boards and onto the rubber carpet atop the ice. I thought he would still be at the arena with my brother. It's why I got my ass up this early in the first place.

"Yes, please!" Mazy says, her tone full of relief. As far as best friends go, she's practically award-winning. But she's not exactly coordinated. Or strong. Or . . . handy.

She's incredibly nice, though. And usually, that's enough for me.

"I got it," Noah says, taking over the weight. His effort makes my side feel lighter too, and the seam between the two pieces is gone now that he's holding them together. It's too bad I have to stand up and look him in the eyes. If I could hammer the pieces together from down here, I wouldn't hate his gesture as much as I'm going to in three, two, one . . .

"That's Mazy, by the way. I know how easily you forget people." I utter the words as I rise, and by the time our eyes meet, my mouth is locked into a hard line.

Noah's nostrils flare with his quiet exhale, and his head tilts slightly.

"I went to Miller Brook, too, Frankie. I know Mazy." He blinks slowly, then rolls his head to turn his attention to my friend. "Hi, Mazy. It's nice to see you."

"Hi, Noah." Mazy's mouth pulls into that tight, embarrassed smile that makes her dimples double and turns her cheeks bright pink. When it comes to Noah Drake, Mazy and I have always agreed on one thing—he's probably the hottest male ever to share our zip code. But where Mazy's crush stopped at looks, mine went a whole lot deeper. I loved the way Noah's voice changed over the years. I felt joy when I heard his laugh. When he got injured his freshman year of college and came home for surgery, I promised not to tell my brother when I saw him cry. And maybe that's why I kept last summer's kiss to myself. Because hot as he may be and as sweet as I always hoped he secretly was, Noah Drake is, in fact, a dog.

"I know who Mazy is," he whispers at me from the other side of the set. I can see half his face peeking around the fake chimney, and I narrow my eyes and stare into his left eyeball. I wish I could reach out and poke it.

"I was being glib." I position a nail against the wood and haul my arm back to give the hammer a swing. I pound it in after three solid smacks.

"Glib. Is that another word for mean?" His voice is low, but not so low that Mazy can't hear bits and pieces of this conversation.

I step back and heave out a short breath before meeting his gaze.

"Yep. It sure is," I say before nodding toward the next portion of the set.

Noah grabs one end while Mazy holds the other, and between the three of us, we manage to steady the largest part of the folding backdrop in place so I can hammer in the last few braces.

"You should consider putting hinges on these for next year," Noah says, tapping his fingertip on the last brace after my final hammer blow.

"That's such a good idea," Mazy beams. I roll my eyes and turn my back to them. The chill in the air is pretty biting, but if I don't get a coat of paint on everything today, it won't be ready in time for our first afternoon open tomorrow.

I crouch down and pop open the lid on the can of bright white before pouring half the gallon into one of the paint pans.

"Hey, Frankie. Since Noah is here now, would you

mind if I took off so I can try to get a few more hours of sleep before the concert tonight?"

My eyes dart to Mazy's face, and she gives me a wry grin as she lifts a shoulder. I dragged her out of bed at seven over winter break, and because she's a good friend, she joined me without griping. And we are going to be out late at the concert tonight.

"Yeah, sure. It's just paint, so I can do it alone if I need to."

I flit my gaze to Noah for a beat. I'm giving him an out, too. I don't need him soothing his guilt by joining me for handiwork.

"Thanks," Mazy breathes out. She leans down to give me a hug, nearly dipping the ends of her blonde braids into the pan of paint. I scoop them up before they run into trouble, and she stares at me with wide eyes and a thankful expression.

"Nice to see you, Noah." Her cheeks flash a bright red, and I swear she's putting extra sway in her hips as she passes him. He holds up a palm and smiles through tightly closed lips.

"Careful. I think she likes you," I say when my friend is far enough away for me to let my snark fly.

"At least one of you does," he grumbles. Our eyes tangle for a second, and eventually, I stand up tall and huff out a short laugh.

"I liked you, too, once." I hold the paint pan out for him to take, along with the brush. His thumb grazes the top of my hand as he takes the brush, and it literally feels like he dragged a magic wand laced with morphine over my skin.

"Only that once, huh?" He quirks a brow, and I look away before I feel that pull he's so good at using to draw me in.

"Yeah, just once. And look what that got me. Kiss 'em and forget 'em! Add me to your ledger, I guess." I cringe at my own words, so I keep my back to him as I unwrap a second brush and hook my finger through the handle on the paint can. I've been holding my hurt in for months. Some petty shit is bound to come out the longer he's around me. I don't like the way it looks on me, though. I'm better than that. Than this.

His silence is a good sign that I caught him off guard with my words and maybe cut him a little too. His flirtatious smirk seems to have faded, and his gaze is lost in the smooth surface of the paint in his hands.

"It goes on the wood. Like in that movie, *The Karate Kid*. Paint the fence?" His eyes blink at me, and I mimic the famous movie scene, drawing my brush up and down in the air. Noah's lip curls, and my stomach rushes with butterflies. That's the dangerous feeling that will get me in trouble, so I cut it short, move to the opposite end of the winter set, and start to paint.

For several minutes, we work in silence, and it's almost nice. The tingles on my skin—the ones I get simply from being near Noah—linger, though. And every time I catch him glancing in my direction, my chest grows warm. I need to remember that this feeling, it's a trick.

He steps back to admire the section he painted, and I

do the same. I think when we add in more of the red and black paint, it will look almost new again.

Noah swaps his white pan for the gallon of red. I get a little stuck watching his forearm muscles as he pries open the lid. Those arms used to be scrawny sticks. Now he's a man.

"Do you have something to cover this with?"

I look away before he turns his attention to me. The last thing I need is him catching me admiring anything and thinking I'm open to messing around.

"No, but it should be fine sitting out for the night. Besides, everyone knows what this place is. You'd have to be a real dick to steal Santa's workshop."

"I meant to protect it from the snow," he explains.

I squint at his words and shift my gaze to him, my mouth contorted to match my skepticism.

"We aren't getting snow for at least two weeks, Noah." It's literally been the lead story on the local news for the last two days. It's rare for us not to have a white Christmas, but according to the forecasters, this holiday is shaping up to be bone dry.

"I don't know," he muses, glancing up at the puffy clouds. He squints from their reflection as he makes a quarter turn, his expression serious. "I feel snow in the next few days."

I study him as he stares up at the blue sky, the sun kissing his golden lashes, and the curled ends of his hair blowing around the hem of his beanie. He's still wearing his gray sweatpants and the blue and gold Tiff University practice jersey, which he fills out a lot more than he did even a year ago. My dad was so proud when Noah and my brother were recruited together. A part of me has always wondered if Noah made the school take Anthony, too, as a condition. My brother is good, but he's not Tiff good. I don't think he's left the bench more than a handful of times over the last two and a half years.

I spare a quick glance at his face one last time, the cut of his jaw, and slight stubble. His beard will grow in over the next two weeks. Of course, he'll be wearing a long, white, fake one most of the time we're together.

"So, this concert—"

He drops his chin, and his gaze lands on me before I have a chance to mask what I fear is one of those ooey, gooey, admiring expressions with doe eyes and parted lips. I call it Noah Drake Face. I've worked so hard to shed it. Like riding a bike, I guess. Slipped right back into practice. And judging by the smirk playing on his lips, Noah caught me.

"You aren't invited," I blurt out. A bit of an overreaction to a question he hasn't even asked, but he caught me ogling.

"Wow, I mean. Okay, then." He holds up his brush in one hand, the can of paint dangling from the other, and slowly backs away from me.

In an attempt to double the space between us, I rush to the other side of the set, brushing my hip along the fresh paint. The denim snags on the particle board as I pass, and I silently pray it's not as bad as it felt, but the white blotch that stretches from the side pocket on my overalls to the edge of the back pocket quashes any hope.

"Damn it!" I set down my can and twist my hips to get a better look at the scope of the damage.

"If you wash it right now, it will come right out. Here," Noah says, setting his paint and brush down and gesturing for me to follow him toward the arena.

I don't want to follow him anywhere, but I also don't want to ruin my favorite piece of clothing.

"Ugh," I grumble, balling my fisted hands to my sides as I follow Noah's lead.

As we near the building, the smacks from sticks slapping at pucks perforate the air, and the scraping sound of skates on ice broken up by periodic whistles fills my ears as soon as Noah swings open the entry door.

"Follow me. Nobody's in the locker room, and I have extra sweats in my bag." Noah keeps walking along the glass, but I pause for a second, not sure I need to be heading into a closed space with him, putting on his clothes.

My brother's voice hits my ears, and I glance toward the ice where he's standing in the middle of the rink, coaching whistle perched on his bottom lip. Anthony looks so much like our dad out there, from his posture to the way he pulls his beanie down low to cover his ears. He's running the winter camp, the same one he and Noah used to participate in when they were young.

"Thirty seconds to catch your breath, then we go again!" He skates along the line of exhausted twelve-year-olds, eying them for strengths and weaknesses. He wants to be a coach when he finishes at Tiff, and though he didn't quite have what it takes to start in college, I think he'll be incredible, leading young players through the ropes.

"Frankie, come on!" Noah whisper-shouts from between the sets of stands. My feet instinctually rush forward, though I haven't quite decided whether to follow him into the locker room.

Noah's gaze bounces between me and my brother, raising his hand after a few seconds and urging me to hurry. By the time I reach him, he's bouncing on his toes like one of the kids waiting in line to see Santa at the photo station.

"Calm down. I'm hurrying," I huff. His hand flattens on my back as I pass him, and he urges me forward, guiding me around a corner and through the locker room door. I spin around the second I'm inside and shove my palms into his chest.

"What the hell, Noah!"

His eyes flash wide, like a mouse trapped in a corner, and he flattens his back against the door.

"Just because nobody's in here doesn't mean *you* should be in here. Can we hurry up?" His eyes somehow widen more through his words, and I glance around the space to see the discarded towels from the men's groups who were in here earlier this morning. The steam from their showers still hangs in the air.

"Point taken," I relent, and his shoulders drop.

"Second row, third locker in. Grab the blue sweats and toss me your pants."

I count my way to his space and chuckle lightly at the unlatched lock dangling from his locker.

"You know the point of a lock is to keep your shit safe," I utter, unhooking the metal from the latch and opening the door. His body wash and a comb sit on the upper shelf, a tan towel dangles from the hook on the back, and a pair of sweats sits neatly folded on the bottom. I pick them up and hold them near my nose to see if there's any hint of his body wash or cologne on the fabric. I feel a little drunk on the scent and once again debate which is more important—my favorite overalls or my resolve.

"You know, I can buy my own ticket, right?"

My brow pulls in and I lean around the corner to glance at him.

"Huh?"

"The concert. It's not like an invite-only thing. I could just buy my own ticket and go." He drops his hands in his pockets and leans his head to the side, his mouth curved a hint. He's challenging me.

I shrug.

"It's country. And I know you hate country. But sure. If you want to spend your money on going to a concert by yourself, have at it." I form a fist and mouth, "Yeah," as I pump it, mocking him.

"I don't hate country."

I chuckle and step back to the hidden space in front of his locker.

"Yeah, okay. Like I said. Have at it." I unhook my overalls and slip the denim down my hips, wrangling my shoes through the legs so I don't have to untie them. My skin beads up from the cold as I stand in my red bikini underwear and a long-sleeved gray shirt.

"Maybe I will," Noah says, his voice sounding closer than before. I clutch his sweatpants in my hands and hold my breath. My gaze drops to my discarded pants, and my pulse throbs in my ears. My eyes flutter shut, and I hover in the land of possibility for a few reckless seconds.

"You got those overalls ready?"

He's right there. Two steps, and I could hand them to him myself, let him get a good look at the body he missed out on. Maybe feel the glow that comes with Noah Drake's attention one last time before I swear it off for good.

I am wet from the thought, and swallow hard.

"Yeah, one second," I say, bending down and snagging my overalls in my free hand.

"Here," I practically croak, tossing them out into the open area and turning my back to the temptation to follow.

I shake out his sweats and gather up one leg at a time, slipping my feet, shoes and all, through the cuffed bottoms. I wriggle them up my hips and roll the top twice at my waist before turning around to find Noah standing at the end of the row, watching me. My pussy gets wetter, and now my nipples are hard. I wish I wasn't wearing this bra so he'd be forced to see them.

"You like the view?" I say in a wry tone. I was right. It feels good to let him look. *Too good.*

"Always have," he says, his words coming quick and easy. His gaze lingers on my hips, and the tip of his tongue slips out between his lips. I hold on to the moment until his eyes lift to meet mine, and when my chest fills with so much chaos it becomes hard to breathe, I end it.

"If you're not going to wash those, give them to me. You can go. I'll see myself out." I hold out my open palm, and Noah's gaze sticks to mine. His mouth curls a hint more, that curled dimple, the backward C, creasing his cheek. I thrust my fingers out wide a few times, urging him to quit playing games. I'm done playing mine, and he finally drops my pants in my hand.

"There's some laundry stuff by the equipment closet in the back. I'll finish up the paint and give you a ride home."

"It's fine. You can leave the rest for me. And I'll just walk," I say, flippantly.

"Frankie, don't be like that. Let me give you a ride home," he says through an exasperated sigh.

I glance at him over my shoulder and smile as I reach the equipment room's closed door.

"I'm not being like anything, Noah. Except myself. Because that's all there is here. There's *me*, and then there's *you*. Two separate things. Not together in any way. Ever."

I twist the knob to open the door and pull the string for the light so I can scan the shelves for soap. I find detergent and grab it before shutting the light off again and closing my heart to any crazy ideas. All the heat from before is gone, and when I turn back around and meet with Noah's soft eyes and drawn-in lips, I am impervious.

"At least let me drive you home."

I pause when I'm parallel with him, turning so our toes nearly meet, and my closed-lip smile widens.

"You worried that magical snowstorm you're predicting will bury me on my way?" I tease.

He blinks slowly and takes away the few remaining inches between us, his nose close enough to graze against mine.

I feel nothing.

I feel nothing.

"I'm not worried, Frankie." He leans in, his chin over my shoulder and his breath hot against my ear. "I am obsessed."

I take in a sharp breath as his chin tickles against the side of my neck. His mouth comes dangerously close to mine, but my eyes remain open—aware. I refuse to blink. Even when his gaze dips to my mouth. And when he presses his tongue to the pad of his thumb. And when . . .

"You got a little paint here," he hums, running his wet thumb from the edge of my bottom lip, down my chin, then slowly along my throat and over my collarbone. His touch grows slower and lighter, but he continues to paint a faint, invisible line down the center of my chest, between my breasts, all the way below my navel until his finger hooks in the front of his sweatpants.

He pauses there, tugging lightly before letting his hand slip away. I refuse to swallow. But I want to.

"You watch, Frankie. It's going to snow this week. I just know it."

I shift my gaze until our eyes are deadlocked. My breathing is measured, but my heart is racing. Is this what it's like being a Noah Drake girl? Constant seduction. Random brushes with heat. Always feeling on the verge of having him feel something back. Always being left wanting more.

He backs away, and I take the reins of breathing my own air again.

"Too bad Santa's got you on the naughty list. Boys like you don't get everything they want, Noah Drake." I purse my lips and hold on to the bitter taste in my mouth. It's the only thing I've got to fend off the waves of desire crashing over me in his wake.

"You forget, Frankie Bardot"—he chuckles lightly and winks as he reaches the door—"I *am* Santa."

And just like good ole St. Nick, he disappears in a flash, and I'm left no longer wanting to kiss this boy but to instead somehow repel him.

3 / noah

I KNEW I should have packed a few more things to bring home over break. Sure, I would have had more laundry to do since literally everything I own up at campus needs a good wash, but at least I wouldn't be sifting through two drawers of jeans and sweatpants and a few hangers of T-shirts and sweaters to find something remotely classy to wear to this concert I'm crashing tonight.

To be fair, going to the concert was Anthony's idea. He's still got a thing for his ex-girlfriend, and he found out she's in town and planning on going. I'm not real keen on flirting with his sister in front of him, but it was hard to turn down his invitation. Especially after accidentally—*maybe not totally accidentally*—catching a glimpse of Frankie in those fucking sexy little panties.

I flip through the hung shirts in my closet one more time, hoping something new will appear this time around. When it doesn't, I give in and head down the hall to my parents' room. My mom sits in the middle of their bed with her laptop and a messy pile of notecards.

"How's the book coming?" I ask as I hang in the doorway.

She pushes her reading glasses down her nose and peers at me over the red rims.

"You know, I think at this rate, I may just finish it within a year. Maybe two." She pulls her glasses off, flips the screen shut, and pushes the computer to her side. She's a legal assistant at a big firm downtown, but she's always dreamed of writing a book. My dad bought her a new laptop for their anniversary two years ago, and she's been pecking out the words for her first novel here and there ever since.

"It's not a race." My words make her mouth inch up on one side. She used to say the same thing to me when I got frustrated while working on my math homework at the kitchen table. I hated that I was stuck working on something I wasn't good at while my friends were outside playing. But some things take time.

"Who made you so smart?"

"This woman who is the next great American author." I get her to blush but also to stand and pull me in for a hug.

"I'm proud of you," I say over her head as she folds into my chest. My height came from my dad's side.

"Thanks, kiddo." She pats my chest softly as she backs away, then looks me up and down. "You look nice."

"Do I?" I quirk a brow and look down at my black

shirt, stuffing the hem into the waist of my dark blue jeans.

"You always look nice in dark colors." She brushes her palm along my right arm a few times, probably removing lint from my mostly sweatshirt wardrobe.

"Thanks. I just wish I brought home a button-down or two. You think I could borrow one of Dad's?" My eyes squint with my question because I hate asking her to dig into his stuff when he's deployed. She never says anything, but I sense that it makes her miss him. My dad's been in Kuwait for nine months. I won't see him until spring break, maybe.

"I know just the one," my mom says, tapping her finger against the center of my chest.

I follow her to the closet, where she pulls out a black fitted button down, the sleeves already unbuttoned and ready to roll up a quarter of my arms. I smirk, seeing the near-permanent creases in the fabric.

"Yeah, I gave up getting him to iron his clothes a long time ago. He says he spends so much time holding an iron for his military uniform that he is protesting all other ironing," she says, pulling it from the hanger and holding it open for me.

"I'm just going to wear it the same way, so it's fine." I pull my T-shirt off and slide my arms in one at a time.

I button it up, leaving the top two undone, and turn to face my mom. Her eyes crinkle at the edges, and she smiles as she straightens the collar and tugs the shirt down at the bottom so it sits just right.

"You look so much like he did at your age. Same size,

too. It's uncanny." Her eyes well up, but I don't say a word, instead letting her wipe the evidence away while I pretend I don't notice.

"Thanks, Mom." I drop my hands in my pockets as she takes a step back. Her eyes flit to mine then back to the center of my chest as she taps a finger to the side of her mouth.

"One last touch," she says, moving to her dresser and opening the top drawer. She pulls out my dad's watch case and opens the lid, pulling out the black and silver Tag Heuer.

"Mom, I can't—"

"*Shh.*" She grabs my wrist and tugs it into her so she can slip the watch around it. "Your dad doesn't care. And it's a nice touch. Besides, you're trying to impress someone. This watch? It's impressive."

"I'm not trying to impress anyone." I pucker my lips and tilt my head a hair, trying to sell the lie. My mom's gaze holds mine, though, and it takes her about two seconds to conclude I'm full of shit.

"Noah, you've been trying to impress that girl since you hit puberty. I wish you realized you didn't have to try so damn hard. Frankie's already impressed. She's been in love with you since sixth grade."

My mouth hangs open just enough to make me look guilty. Because I *am* guilty. But I don't think I've been as obvious as my mom says. I didn't start to think of Frankie in *that* way until high school.

"I don't think it's like that, Mom. It's just nice to see her. It's been a while and—"

"And since you kissed her this summer, things are . . . different?" She quirks a brow and knocks me back a step with that hammer drop only she can give.

"How—?" *She saw that?*

"I was on the couch by the window, working on my book. And you guys didn't exactly hide it. You stopped under the streetlight." She shrugs one shoulder and flashes a knowing, one-sided smile.

I run my palm down my face, then pinch the bridge of my nose, relenting to the fact that my mom always knows everything.

"Pretty sure I blew it after that," I admit. Might as well get some advice from an expert on forgiveness. My dad is a big romantic, but he's not great at remembering things—like anniversaries, birthdays, and dinner plans.

"I'm pretty sure you know how to get the girl, Noah. I'm not naïve. And I see the comments on your social media."

My neck heats at the thought of my mom seeing the love I get from female fans. Sometimes they don't keep the overt propositions like the one I got yesterday to my DMs. But I never really brought my high school girlfriends home to meet my parents for dinner or anything. I mean, I snuck a few into my room, and I definitely went on "camping trips" in the Bronco.

"Just be yourself. That's the guy Frankie grew up making starry eyes at."

I nod and wear a polite smile, but I'm not so sure being myself is going to cut it. And then there's Anthony.

"I don't think Anthony wants her making starry eyes at me."

"Well, Anthony doesn't get to decide who his sister looks at or how." My mom shrugs and moves back to her bed, pulling her computer onto her lap and gathering the spread-out notecards into a neat pile.

She has a point. Also, it's not her face that would get bashed in by his fist. Or his friendship lost. We've got the rest of the season, too, and we're still roommates at the house by campus. He made it pretty clear he doesn't want me fucking up his sister's life.

But it's not like she would up and change colleges now, especially since I won't be at Tiff after this year. And my mom has a point; Frankie makes her own decisions. But so do I.

"Be myself, huh?"

"Yep," my mom says, sliding her glasses back in place as she opens her computer again. Then, with a wave of her hand, she shoos me out the door.

I manage to keep the confidence she injected into me roaring through my veins as Anthony and I drive to the amphitheater. A group of women gathered at the beer tent give me long, hard stares, which helps to lift my shoulders and broaden my chest.

By the time Frankie shows up with Mazy, I'm ripe with self-sureness. And the second Anthony ditches me to go find his ex in the sea of blankets and chairs, I gulp down the rest of my beer and head toward Frankie at the merch stand.

"You'd look good in that one," I say, my chin just over

The Goalie and Santa's Little Helper

her shoulder as I point at the white T-shirt with the sunset image emblazoned on the chest.

"You just like that it's white, and you can get it wet," she shoots back. There's a playfulness in her voice, though, and that gives me courage.

"I'm not saying I *wouldn't* like that," I admit.

"*Pfft.*" She rolls her head away from me and crosses her arms over her chest. She's wearing a slim gray sweater with silver woven down the sleeves in a criss-cross pattern. It stops right at her waist, where the tight jeans take over and tuck into a pair of knee-high black boots. My hands ache to trace along the curve of her hips.

"What will it be, miss?" The merch guy notices the same curves I just did, and when his gaze shifts to me, I flash a quick sneer.

"Do you have the white one in medium?"

I let out a short, quiet laugh, and Frankie's head swivels so our eyes meet.

"I was going to pick that one anyway!"

"Sure, you were," I tease.

Her eyes dim and she turns her attention back to the middle-aged man at the counter.

"Actually, wait. I'll take the hoodie, in large."

He nods and heads to the large box in the back to pull out a dark blue hoodie. A dull pain swells where my ribs meet, like a hole in my stomach.

"You didn't have to do that to prove something. I know you want the white one." Frankie loves sunsets, and the design looks like her style. That's why I predicted she'd pick it. Not because it's white, and I'm a pervert. But it is white, and I am a pervert. I can't really ignore the facts.

"I can always use another sweatshirt. The shore gets cold." She shrugs and holds the hoodie against her chest after the man hands it to her.

"Perfect," she says. She fishes a credit card from her back pocket, but as she moves to hand it to the man, I push her hand down and meet her gaze.

"I got this. I insist."

She blinks, and I'm not sure whether it's because she's surprised or is buying time to come up with an argument.

"Fine," she relents, putting her card away and leaving me to close out the bill at the stand as she marches toward Mazy.

"I'll take the white one in medium too," I say. He chuckles, probably amused at what a sucker I am. He snags the shirt for me and runs my card while I roll it up and tuck it under my arm.

The sound of tuning guitar strings reverberates throughout the amphitheater as I turn and scan the crowd. I'm not standing quite as tall as before, but I'm not giving up yet. I pull my phone from my pocket when it buzzes. It's Anthony, messaging to get two more beers and meet him on the other side of the lawn. Apparently, he found Gemma, and she said we could sit with her and her friends on their blanket.

Great.

I send back a thumbs up and fill my lungs with one more deep breath to ready my ego for one last try—at least for tonight. I spot Mazy and Frankie standing in the beer line and breathe out a quiet "Thanks" to the universe for putting me in the right place at the right time for once. I step up behind them and softly clear my throat.

"Are you following me?" Frankie flips around so we're toe-to-toe when she glares up at me.

I offer a tight-lipped smile and let my head fall to one side as I hand her the shirt she really wanted. She takes a half-step back as her eyes drop to it, and her lips part with a quick breath.

"Olive branch?" I give her a sheepish smile.

She takes the shirt and unrolls it to expose the design.

"It suits you," I say, keeping the devilish smile from before in check and instead meeting her gaze with my own to convince her of my sincerity. "And I mean because it's really pretty."

She sucks in her lips, seeming to be fighting a smile.

"Thank you," she utters.

I lean in, but not as close as before.

"You're welcome."

Our eyes dance for a moment, Frankie working hard not to let her mouth betray her by curling up at the edges, me keeping mine shut so stupid words don't fly out of it.

"Cute shirt!" Mazy squeals, taking it in her hands and holding it up to fully inspect it.

I order four beers while her friend has her distracted. I hand Frankie two of them, and when she reaches into her pocket for her phone, I assume to send me cash, I shake my head.

"Let me buy a cute girl a cute shirt and a drink," I say,

loud enough Mazy hears it this time. She holds her palm over her mouth and stares at her friend with wide eyes.

"I hope you know this doesn't mean you get to be late for your shift tomorrow," Frankie says as I walk away.

I spin around and walk backward so I can keep my eyes on her for a few more seconds. I'm going to endure two hours of country music, but the last fifteen minutes made it all worthwhile.

"Santa's never late." I wink, then pray she doesn't roll her eyes and call me a cheesy loser. When she holds the lip of her beer against her mouth in a poor attempt to shield her grin, I turn back toward the crowd and scan the sea of heads in search of her brother's blue ballcap. I spot him and weave my way through the crowd, eating my own stupid grin well before I have to face him. But I keep an eye on the cute girl in silver and blue jeans swaying her hip about a hundred yards away for the rest of the night.

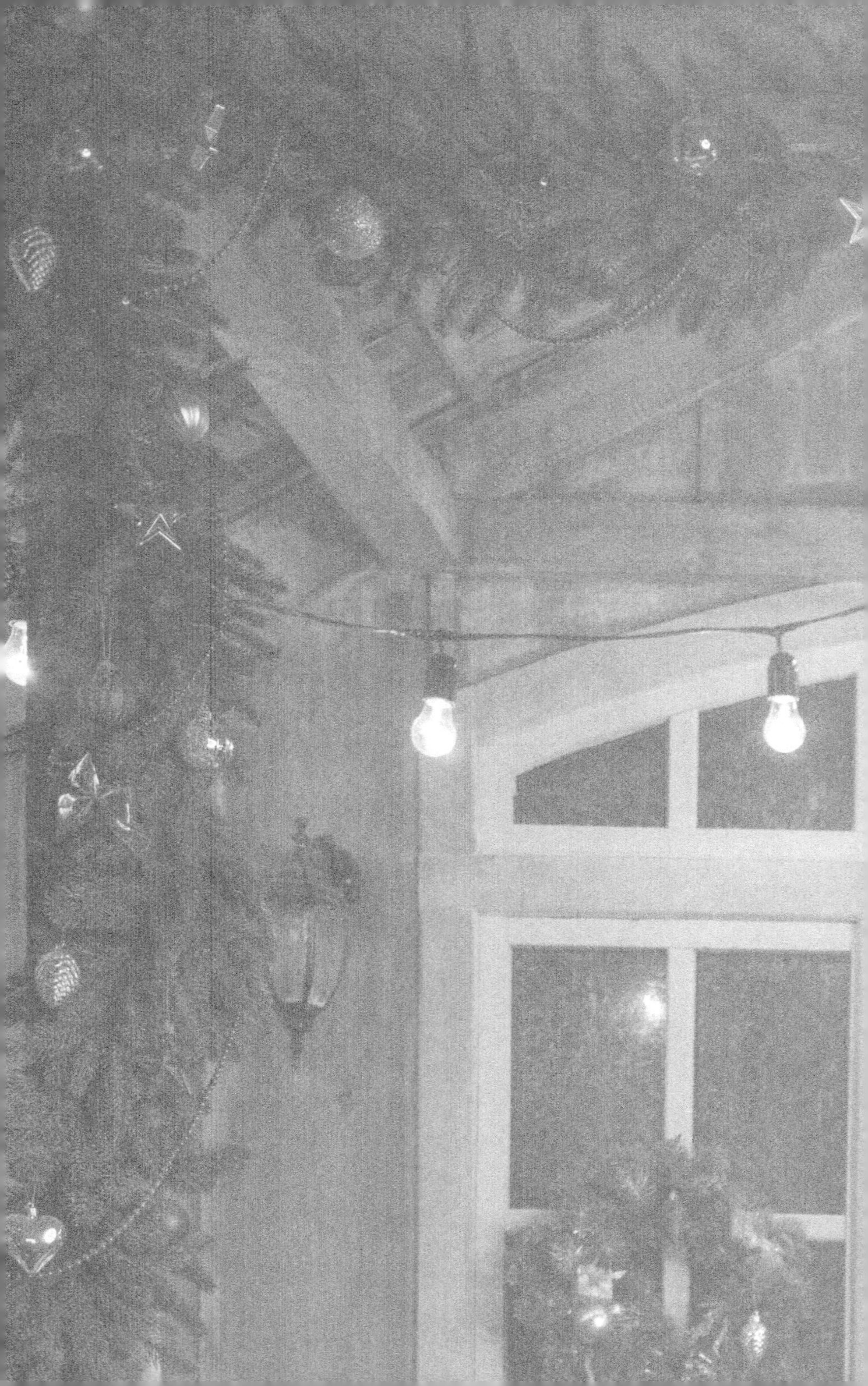

4 / frankie

THE FRESHMAN FIFTEEN IS LEGIT.

I've been away at college for five months, and in that time, my jeans have gotten a little tighter, and a few of my favorite sweaters hug my chest with a little more . . . *curve*. As a girl who has always worn B cups but got to buy her first Cs, I haven't minded the extra weight up top so much. But as I try to slide into my holiday skating dress for the photo booth, those extra curves are making the cut a little more revealing.

"Just don't pick anything up in front of anyone and you should be fine," Mazy advises through the crunch of pretzels she's stuffing into her mouth.

I spin around and face her in my kitchen, having just bent down to pluck my meal prep container from the bottom shelf of the fridge.

"Is it that bad?" I wince.

She pauses with her half-eaten pretzel an inch from her lips.

"I mean, bad is subjective. You'll probably get a lot more tips."

I cover my face with my hands and groan.

"It's not that bad, Frankie."

I peel a few of my fingers away to glare at her.

"I literally have to pick small children up all afternoon to help them onto Santa's lap." *And Santa happens to be the one guy I want to be modest in front of most.*

"Maybe wear bloomers underneath," she says.

My chin drops to my chest, and I shudder with a short, frustrated laugh.

"I'm *wearing* bloomers." I lift my skirt to reveal very short shorts, shifting my hip to the side so she can see how high up they ride.

She chuckles.

"All I'm saying is, I wish I looked like that in bloomers." She pops another pretzel in her mouth, the crunch irritating me now.

"Yeah, well, I'm not at the club. I'm at Santa's Workshop." I shimmy my skirt down as low as it will ride on my hips. Because the outfit is basically a one-piece, though, it rides up the second I lift my arms again.

"That's it. I'm putting sweatpants on underneath," I grumble, moving toward the stairs. Mazy grabs my wrist and stops me before I get too far. She levels me with a wry smirk and a hard stare.

"Are you afraid of being feminine in front of strangers, or are you afraid of being sexy in front of Noah Drake?"

I exhale and let my gaze wander to the side as I chew at the inside of my mouth.

"A little of both. But mostly, looking like *this*—" I fluff up my skirt up with my hands. "In front of Noah."

My friend takes both of my hands in hers and shakes them twice.

"I'm your best friend, Frankie. And I will never lie to you. Agreed?"

I nod, knowing she's ninety-nine percent genuine. She would spare my feelings with a small, meaningless fib, but only rarely. Mazy has always told me the truth. She's also told me everything. Which makes the fact I haven't told her about the kiss sit even heavier in my stomach.

"Will you maybe get some extra looks from a handful of dads who show up tonight? Probably. Some moms? Maybe. It will be brief and quickly forgotten. But when it comes to making an impression on Noah, one that he will etch into his memory and torture himself with all winter long? That's a definite yes. Miller Brook's favorite playboy goalie will be obsessed. And if one of us has a chance to bring that boy to his knees, I say we take it."

I hold her gaze for a beat and consider that word choice—*obsessed*. Noah said he was as much. I figured he was simply trying to get under my skin, but maybe he truly does regret how he left things between us this summer. I wouldn't mind torturing him a little more, let him really see what he missed out on, what he could have had.

"You're right," I finally say, squeezing her hands before letting go to gather my keys, phone, water bottle, and afternoon snacks into a small backpack.

"That's my girl!"

Mazy follows me out the door, heading to her car, which is parked on the street. She pulls the bright yellow sailor hat from her back pocket and clips it to her hair to hold it in place. She's working at the custard stand downtown over the holiday break, and as self-conscious as I may be about wearing this short, green costume dress, she's the exact opposite, wearing her bright yellow egg-shaped outfit loud and proud.

I snag my skates from the garage and rush to my car in the driveway, dumping my blades and backpack on the backseat floor before sliding into the driver's seat and cranking the engine to get the heat going. I rub my hands together in front of the vent and remind myself there are heaters near the photo booth, and the nylon tights I'm wearing will help stave off some of the chill after a lap or two around the rink.

After a quick touch-up of my lipstick and double check of my lashes and hair, I pull out of our neighborhood and make my way to the workshop set. I spot Noah's Bronco near the arena, where he's skating with my brother. I check my watch, noting he still has five minutes before he's late. Not that I have any recourse, or am even his boss. At least not formally. This is my project, though. I started it, and the community center has come to count on the funds raised to buy extra food to feed the low-income seniors and members of our community every Christmas Eve. There is no way I'm letting Noah mess that up.

I set my backpack into the small lockbox behind the background, then sit on top of it, using it as a bench as I lace up my skates. It's been a while since I've taken to the ice. My North Carolina campus doesn't have the same easy access to ice for skating. I find my balance and slowly glide out to the middle of the rink, moving to the left and right until I find my usual rhythm and pick up speed. After a lap, I test my legs and shift to skate backward. I've never been more than a novice at figure skating, but by the end of last winter, I was able to do a slow spin and single axel. Granted, my arms usually flail aimlessly at my sides to maintain my balance. I might score a two, maybe a two and a half, in a competition. But I can land it—most of the time.

With my second lap under my belt and my legs finally warm, I bend my knees and stretch out my arms, then take a deep breath and push up from the ice. My toe pick catches the ice three quarters of the way through my turn, sending me into an awkward cartwheel-turned-summersault. I slide a dozen feet on my knees before finally coming to a stop and flopping on my ass. The cold bites hard.

"Oh, damn!" I shout, brushing ice from my knees and checking my tights for holes.

"You might be a bit rusty for tricks," Noah says as he slides to a stop at my side. He kneels and holds out a hand.

I'm sure I'm a million shades of red, and not from frostbite. My face is hot, and I feel incredibly foolish. Plus, the skirt I was so worried about before is hiked up to my hips, and the crotch on my bloomers is cutting deep.

"Yeah, I forgot that skating isn't quite like riding a

bike," I whine, taking Noah's hand and grabbing hold of his bicep with my other.

"Yeah, it's like riding a bike . . . on ice," he says through a deep chuckle.

My eyes scan his legs as he helps me up, the red velvet of the Santa pants now damp and crusted with ice at the knees. As he hoists me to a complete stand, I fall into his chest, my feet skipping along the slick surface in a fury to find my balance. Noah's hands drop to my waist, and he steadies me as he widens his stance.

"Whoa, you okay?" He dips his chin and meets my gaze.

I blink a few times, my focus still on the ice between us. His fingers at my chin, he nudges my face up until our eyes meet. His cheeks dimple with his smile, his breath a short laugh. I'm so embarrassed.

"I'm okay," I breathe out, breaking our connection and pushing away from his steady hold.

I skate to the workshop without trying anything fancy and snag the small hand towel I left behind after yesterday's painting session. I use it to brush the ice from my costume, then toss it to Noah as he skates up. He brushes off his knees, then tosses it back to me. It's then I realize he's not wearing a shirt under the fluffy red coat. His chest is on full display, all the way down to his belly button. And a little lower.

"Umm, it's not really Magic Mike Meets Santa," I say, gesturing to his exposed body and trying like hell not to swallow the sudden lump in my throat. He's in better shape than I remember. Are these the same washboard abs he had at the lake over the summer? No wonder I let him kiss me. And kissed him back.

"I was still kinda hot from skating sprints. I'll button up when we get our first visitors."

I nod before turning my back to him and mumbling quietly, "Or you could button up now so I don't have to work so hard not to like you."

"Huh?"

Shit. He heard that.

"Nothing," I say, glancing over my shoulder. His smirk confirms my hunch.

If I'm going to get through the next two weeks, I need to focus on the job. Maybe Mazy was right, and we'll end up getting more tips. Perhaps we'll get a few adults and some of the college kids up on Santa's lap. I mean, who can resist a sexy Santa and a naughty elf in a short skirt?

I punch the code into the lockbox and move my backpack aside so I can take out the box of tiny candy canes I stocked in here yesterday. I'm steadier on the rubber mat, so I stick to it while I rip open the package and avoid the ice until I have to skate around the photo backdrop and flip on the lights.

"I forgot how cool you make this look," Noah says, hands on his hips, Santa coat still wide open.

I clear my throat and utter, "Thanks."

His lip ticks up on one side when my gaze drops to the center of his chest.

"Guess it's time to button up, huh?" He starts at the bottom, working his way up—slowly.

"You know, you can wear a shirt under that," I mutter,

moving back to the mat to turn on the blow-up reindeer and giant, glowing presents.

"It was sweaty. I'll plan better tomorrow. I'm sorry."

I glance over my shoulder, his chin tucked as he works the last button in place and pulls the fake beard from his pocket.

"It's okay," I say, not quite loud enough for him to hear. A part of me doesn't want to let him off the hook. I'm sure he was sweaty after skating for the last two hours, but I also think he flaunted his bare chest in front of me on purpose.

"Hey, Frankie. You want me to set up like we did last year?" Norris Gibson's grizzled voice fills my lungs with air. Part of it is relief that it's no longer just Noah and me, but mostly I'm elated by the familiar warmth I get when I'm around the man who used to coach my dad back when he played hockey.

"Aww, it's great to see you," I say, hobbling toward the older man in the gray wool pageboy hat. I welcome his hug with my own, embracing him and inhaling the sweet scent of expensive cigar that always sticks to his scraggly beard. It's his only indulgence. He's been a fixture at our local newspaper for forty years. High school hockey coaching was his side gig.

"Always my favorite part of the year. You know, one of the younger photographers at the paper volunteered to work the booth this year, but I flexed my seniority." He coughs out a laugh as Noah steps up to take his gear bag from him.

"Well, I didn't know we had a celebrity Santa this year.

Good to see you, Noah." He cups Noah's free hand in both of his, giving him an exaggerated shake.

"Yeah, I sort of fell into the gig," he says, his eyes darting to me for a beat. I think he's waiting for me to tattle on him, but I'm over the shock of it all. If he needs volunteer hours for school, I guess this makes sense. It's really his only free time, and my dad does deserve a boys' trip.

"He gave my dad the season off so he could golf," I add. Noah's lips curve a tick, and I think that shade of pink on his cheeks is the guilty kind. He bends down to open Norris's gear bag and begins constructing his light kit.

"That's awful nice. Wonder if he'll regret that after the first kid pees his pants," Norris chuckles.

Noah's head pops up, his guilty smirk replaced by wide eyes and an open mouth.

"Wait, what?"

I wave my hand at him and lower myself to my knees so I can help twist the support beams together.

"It rarely happens. Maybe once or twice," I say.

"Oh, that's better. Wait . . . do you mean, like, ever? Or a season?"

I bite my bottom lip and shift my gaze to Norris. He can't contain his big belly laugh. He pats Noah on the shoulder a few times and waddles his way toward the Santa chair, still chuckling. Noah leans over the gear, close to me.

"Why is he laughing?"

I suck in my lips, trying to hold my own laugh in now.

"He means once or twice a day," I admit, wincing as my shoulders hike.

"Son of a—"

Noah drops the light stand on the bag and stands, stretching his arms over his head and threading his hands behind his neck as he paces along the mat, then steps on the ice.

"I figured my dad would have told you," I holler.

He holds out a thumb, but his mouth is a tight line, and he's beginning to skate a bit faster. He always does that when someone makes him mad on the ice. It's a trick my dad taught him to work out frustrations and cool his temper.

"Think he knows we're exaggerating and teasing him?" Norris laughs out as he rests on the velvet tufted chair.

I shrug.

"He could use a little humbling."

After a few laps, Noah joins me to finish setting up the lighting kit. Norris tests out his framing, adjusting his tripod a few times before ordering Noah to take a seat on the throne. It's strange seeing him sit in that chair. So much of him reminds me of my dad, but there are a lot of things that are not my father at all. Things that could get me in trouble—like the way his hands flex on the chair's arms and how the red pants stretch around his thighs. And my dad's skates are old and scuffed, but Noah's are a sleek black.

"Frankie, you mind playing bratty kid for me for a second?" Norris asks as he points with his hand above the camera, his face pressed against the viewfinder.

"Like, on his lap?"

Noah's chuckle is clear.

"Yeah, just for a few test shots. It's not like you don't know each other."

My mouth straightens, and my stomach twists. Yeah, we know each other. We've kissed. And I've fantasized. And apparently, Noah's now obsessed. The thought of sitting on that lap, with those legs . . .

I swallow hard.

"Sure," I croak.

I take baby steps toward Noah, partly stalling. His cocky smirk doesn't help matters, but then he takes my hand, and his palm is so warm. His grip is strong but gentle, and the touch of his other hand around my waist is firm and proper. The thought of his hand lowering on my leg flashes through my mind as I spin around and skootch my way onto his lap.

"Sorry, I'm heavier than a toddler," I grumble.

Noah's hands find my waist again, and he pulls me into him until my back hits his chest.

"You're perfect," he says at my ear. His breath is warm, and it tickles against my neck. I reach up to adjust my hair, pulling some of it over my shoulder as a shield. When I drop my hands to my lap, though, Noah brushes the locks back over my shoulder, exposing my skin to him again. The shivers down my arm and spine happen instantly.

"Is the beard okay?" he asks.

I twist and crane my neck to look at him. Our mouths are inches apart, and my gaze drops from his eyes to his mouth just as his tongue peeks out. I reach up to tug the beard a little to test how much it moves. His full lips stretch with his smile, and I get a glimpse of his dimple when I pull the beard out a little more.

"You might be in trouble with the skeptical kids. But they'll be excited that Santa's a famous college hockey player, so I guess it's fine."

He breathes out a short laugh, and our gazes lock again. Diamonds light up in his pupils as Norris tests his flash. Our connection doesn't break, even though Noah's probably a little blind right now.

"I'm not famous," he says.

My mouth twists, and I squint my left eye.

"You're a little famous. You have a fandom. They're . . . very aggressive."

His mouth draws in tight, and his chest fills with a long draw of air.

"Yeah, well, I didn't pick those fans. I'm more interested in the scouts. And a certain elf."

My body warms. Damn him, he's so charming. He's such a flirt, which I have always known. But when those powers are focused on me? He makes it really hard to keep my guard up.

"I'm not an elf," I explain. "I'm Santa's helper."

My eyes flutter closed when I realize that doesn't sound much better. In fact, it sounds a lot worse, given this situation. Noah's body quakes with his silent laughter and I turn to face Norris again. My brows lift high.

"We about done here?"

He holds up a finger.

"Yeah, it looks good. Let me just get one good one of

The Goalie and Santa's Little Helper

you two, my gift to your parents. Moms always love this stuff."

I grumble and wriggle a few inches down Noah's thigh.

"I don't think they care—"

"Yeah, that'd be great," Noah contradicts, pulling me back into him.

"Great. One second," Norris says, adjusting his lens and checking the settings on his laptop. He has it set up to a small printer so we can send people home with their shots.

I twist my head to my side, stopping when I feel the curls of Noah's fake beard against my cheek.

"You're loving this, aren't you?"

He shifts under me as his lips hover at my neck.

"Yes." The word comes out slow and smooth, like a long pour of expensive bourbon. It's enough to make my heart kick and tingles run down my arms and legs, wrapping around my thighs and pushing me to squirm a little in his lap.

And then I feel him. He lets out a ragged breath against my neck, and his nose grazes my skin. He's so hard right now, and I'm sitting in a very powerful position.

"Oh!" I say, letting delight color my tone and outweigh the threat of embarrassment.

I cross my legs, pressing my ass into him more, and his forehead falls against my cheek.

"If you want me to get up when we're done, Frankie, you better—"

I shift again, feeling him flex under my ass cheek, and now I'm a little turned on.

"You don't have to get up for a while. You'll be fine."

He exhales into the curve of my neck, reigniting the goose bumps I just tamed. The fingers on his left hand dig into my hip, and his other hand covers my folded ones above my knee. He coaxes our tethered hands upward, stopping at the hem of my short skirt right at the curve of my hip.

"Will you be fine?" he hums.

"Okay, look up here. And smile, you two," Norris says, barely breaking through the bubble I've formed around Noah and me.

I force my mouth into a wide smile and brighten my eyes, which desperately want to flutter closed again now that Noah has shifted his legs and pressed himself directly against my aching center.

The flashes blind me, but I wouldn't have been able to see straight anyhow. Because no—I'm not fine. I'm far from it. And I'm kind of okay with that.

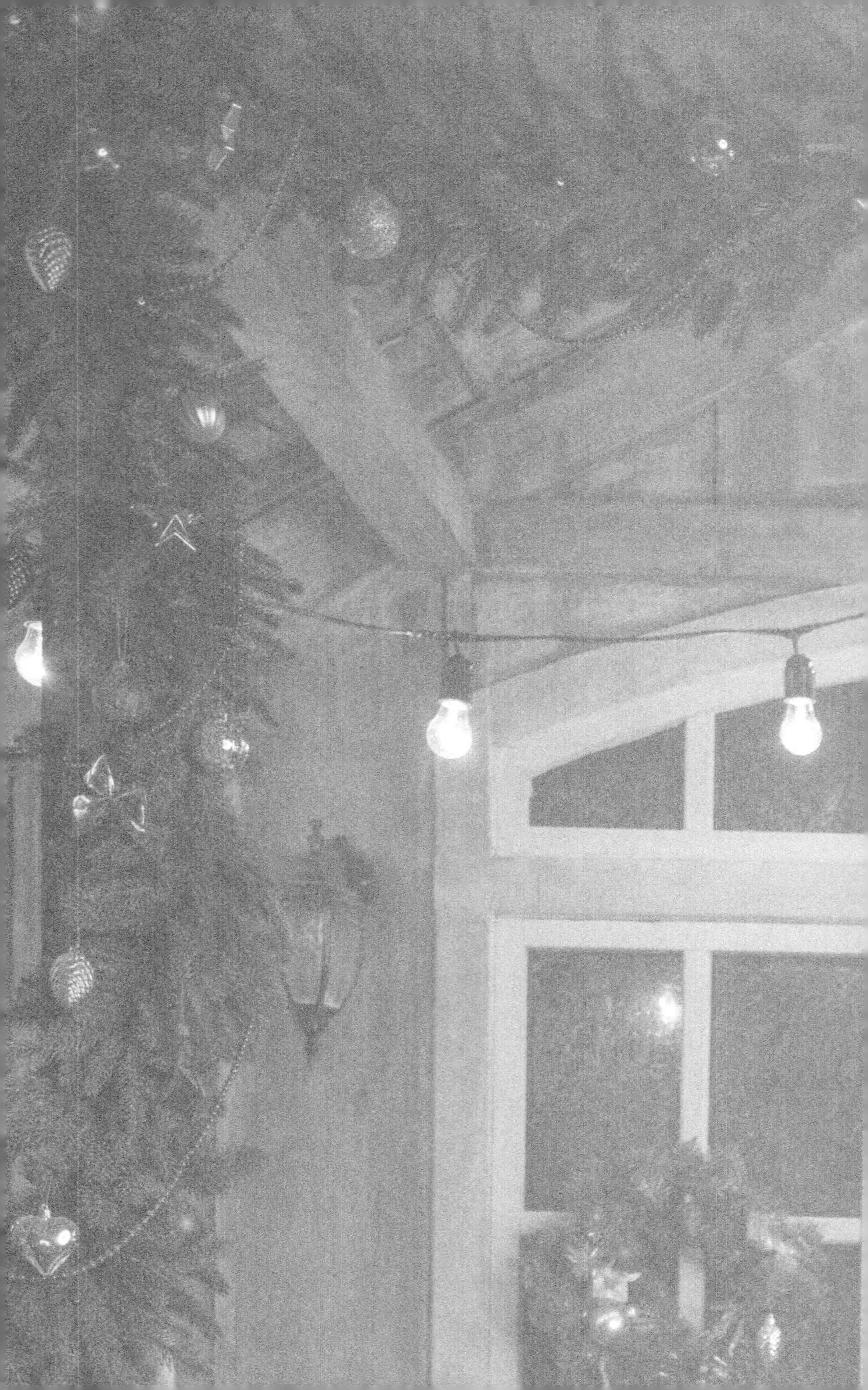

5 /
frankie

THE FIRST WEEK of the photo booth is usually slow. Kids are just getting out of school, parents are balancing holiday duties with work duties, and grandparents aren't in town yet. Normally, our first customers are couples looking for cute holiday photos, or older couples reliving their youth and getting into the Christmas spirit.

But now that the booth has been around for a few years and word has spread, our opening day was one for the record books. I can't tell whether Noah is exhausted or regretful that he signed up for a rigorous unpaid job during his break. Anthony told me that a few of the other guys they graduated high school with got home today, and they plan on watching the Bears game at McGinnie's tonight with all-you-can-eat wings and pints. I'm sure Noah's anxious to get out of here. He hasn't let those cracks show to the kids, though. Not once.

"Ho ho ho!"

My cheeks ache as I smile. I can't help it. From the first

time Noah put on the voice and practiced his belly laugh, it's sparked a massive grin on my face every time. I never would have guessed, but he's really good at this.

"And what's your name?"

It's the last kid for the night. I hung the closed sign by the rink entrance. I think Noah's really putting on a show for this kid since he waited for nearly an hour to see him.

"I'm Conner," the kid answers, a faint whistle capping off his words thanks to the slight split between his two front teeth.

"And how old are you?" Noah asks, tilting his head to the side and giving Conner a good look. We came up with this trick about halfway through the night.

"Wait, don't tell me. I remember you." Noah runs his hand over his beard as a skeptical smirk inches up Conner's face.

"Oh, yeah?" the boy says. He's six. I know because I got the details from his dad and passed them on to Noah through the earbud I buried in his Santa hat.

"You're Conner Graham. And you are pretty tall for a six-year-old," Noah says.

Conner's mouth falls open, and I hold my fist against my smiling lips. This will never get old.

"Thanks for that," Conner's dad says at my side.

"Of course! We like raising money for the community center, but we love making kids smile even more," I say.

"I'm pretty thankful for both. That Christmas Eve dinner is going to be a bright spot for us this year."

The man sinks his hands into his jean pockets as he hikes his shoulders in a shiver. The breeze has kicked up so much that I took Norris up on his offer to wear his bowling league jacket. I think it's more than the cold eating at Conner's dad, though. And since Noah has Conner talking up a storm right now, I breathe in a deep dose of courage to pry into things that aren't my business.

"Things are tight?"

I keep my voice low so Conner can't hear us talk. His father nods, his gaze dropping to the ground, and he kicks at the wet spots on the mat from our long night of customers.

"They furloughed at my company, and my wife is only part-time right now since our daughter just turned one." His shoulders hike with a short, breathy laugh, the kind not meant for something funny.

"She earns just enough to cover the daycare some weeks. It all feels kind of pointless."

I reach into my apron, retrieve the ten dollar bill he gave to me a few minutes ago, and move to hand it back. He shakes his head, however, taking a half step back and lodging his hands deeper in his pockets.

"No, ma'am, that donation is what I can afford. And we'll eat plenty at the community dinner," he says, his smile struggling to reach his eyes.

"It doesn't feel right," I say.

He shakes his head again.

"It wouldn't feel right not to chip in."

I draw in a deep breath, my chest tight. I understand his perspective. I just wish I could do more.

Conner's laughter peels our attention back to him. Norris must have overheard our conversation because he snapped a few candid shots while Noah and Conner were high-fiving. I catch him printing the extras out beyond the father's shoulder. I nod and smile when he slips them into the envelope.

"Well, did you ask Santa for anything special?" his dad asks, scooping his son up and hoisting him onto his hip.

"I told him about the hockey stick I saw and maybe a new jersey." His words end with a whistle.

"Oh, well. Hopefully they can get that at the North Pole. If not, I'm sure he'll get you something just as great," the man says, his gaze catching mine.

"Yeah. Of course he will, because he's Santa!" Conner's fist jets in the air, and his dad pushes his tight smile a little higher.

"Thank you all," the man says, taking the envelope from Norris and nodding a silent thanks to me before shaking Noah's hand.

"Man, that kid was cool," Noah says as the father and son walk along the red carpet that leads to the exit.

"Hockey fan, huh?" I assume.

"HUGE hockey fan!" Noah stretches his arms out for emphasis.

My heart sinks, and I must be wearing the dejection on my face because the second Noah's eyes meet mine, he drops his arms to his sides. His brow pulls in tight.

"What's wrong?"

I glance back toward the parking lot, checking to make sure Conner and his dad are well out of range.

"How expensive is that hockey stick he wants?" I'm

honestly considering clearing out some of my summer job savings to buy it for him.

"I think it's going for three hundred, maybe three-fifty. But it's too big for him anyhow. I think the junior version is half that."

Half that is still a lot.

"Oh," I let slip out, my tone reflecting the lump of coal forming in my chest.

Noah's gaze drifts beyond me to the lot where the man is cranking the engine on a minivan, turning it over three times before it catches into a steady idle. His jaw seesaws as the crease between his brows deepens. I reach for his wrist, circling it with my hand, and his eyes instantly rush back to me.

"You made Conner very happy, and seeing Conner happy made his dad happy." My hand slides down until our palms connect, and our fingers weave together loosely. It doesn't feel forbidden until Noah's gaze drops to our touch. Then his hand is suddenly amazingly warm, and the feeling crawls up my arm into my chest, nearly exploding when his fingers flex between mine and his grasp grows tighter.

"We should close up. I'm sure my brother is waiting for you so he can hit the pub for the game. It's probably the second quarter by now."

I stretch my fingers and wriggle my hand from his hold. The way his fingertips rake along my skin as if he's given up and decided to fall from the cliff he's been clinging to makes my chest burn. Then he bites his bottom lip as his gaze lingers on mine. I should look away, but I don't.

Our trance is finally broken by the sound of metal clanking against ice. We both turn to look at the now-dented light kit lying in two pieces about a foot off the mat.

"Shoot, that's not good," Norris says, his palm working at the grizzly beard on his chin.

"It's my fault. I should have helped you," I say, rushing over to skate onto the ice and grab the few screws that bounced out of reach.

"Ehh, I should know better than to try to do two things at once. I can patch it up before tomorrow. Should be fine."

I hand Norris three screws and a bolt, and he drops them in his pocket. Noah packs the rest of the camera gear while Norris hands me the various pieces of the busted light and stand as he dismantles it carefully. After Noah and I pull our skates off, the three of us shuttle the pieces out to his car for the night.

"I feel bad about that. I think that's his own equipment," I say as Noah and I watch Norris's taillights fade.

The air is crisp enough that I can see my breath. I form an O and puff out a cloud of white fog that glows under the new LED park lights. My lips tingle, but not from the chill. This vibration is from knowing Noah and I are completely alone. Our vehicles are the only two left. Skating rentals at the rink shut down thirty minutes ago, and a park ranger won't be here to lock up the gates for at least an hour.

I swallow down the dry lump that is continuously reforming as Noah shifts his weight, digging the toes of his shoes into the frost-covered pavement. He draws a half circle with a sharp edge, like half a heart, and I hold my breath, hoping he'll finish it. Instead, he erases it with his other foot, adjusts the weight of his duffel, and skates slung over his opposite shoulder.

"One down, eleven more shifts to go," I say, mostly to break the awkward silence. My heart is thundering so loud, I fear Noah can hear it.

His lip tugs up on one side as he drops his chin and pivots his head until our eyes meet.

"It wasn't so bad."

I focus on his lips through the brief stream of fog that escapes with his words. No wonder he was the best kiss I ever had. Just look at that mouth.

"You ready?" I tilt my head to the side toward my car.

"Sure," he hums, shifting the weight of his bag and dragging his slide shoes along the ground. His socks are Tiff University blue with a tiny yellow lightning bolt on the toes. Such a big man for such adorable socks. I smile to myself.

Noah tugs my backpack from my shoulder when we reach my car, opening the driver's side door for me, then dumping my bag in the back seat. His massive body, draped in red velvet and white fur, hovers in the tight space between the open door and my left thigh, and I can't stop envisioning what might happen if I were to simply step one foot out and touch his chest.

"Drive safe, okay? I can't handle the line of irritable parents by myself," he says. He takes a step back, and a rush of cool air fills the void. I glance to my arm and realize I'm still wearing Norris's coat.

"Oh, no!"

I tug at the sleeve, staring at it while I chew at the inside of my cheek.

"I know where he lives. I can drop it off on my way home," Noah offers.

I squint as I glare up at him.

"Are you sure?"

He nods, holding out his hand.

I shimmy the coat from my arms and slip it around my body before handing it to him. He folds it over his arm, then raps his fingers against the edge of the door.

"Same time tomorrow?" he asks.

"Yeah."

It feels like we're stalling. I'm willing to admit *I'm* stalling. And everything in my gut says Noah is too. I hate that it feels so good to be nervous in his presence. I chased this feeling for nearly half my life, clamoring for him to glance my way, or to honor me with a silly compliment about a new pair of shoes or the color of my prom dress.

"Good night, Noah." I reach for the door myself and tug it shut. Because if I leave things to him, I have a feeling we would spend half the night floundering around a real conversation in the middle of a parking lot.

Unless, of course, he asked me to stand and face him.

And then ran his palm along my cheek, brushing the small hairs from my skin with the pad of his thumb. Then leaned in and kissed me. Again. Just the way he did before.

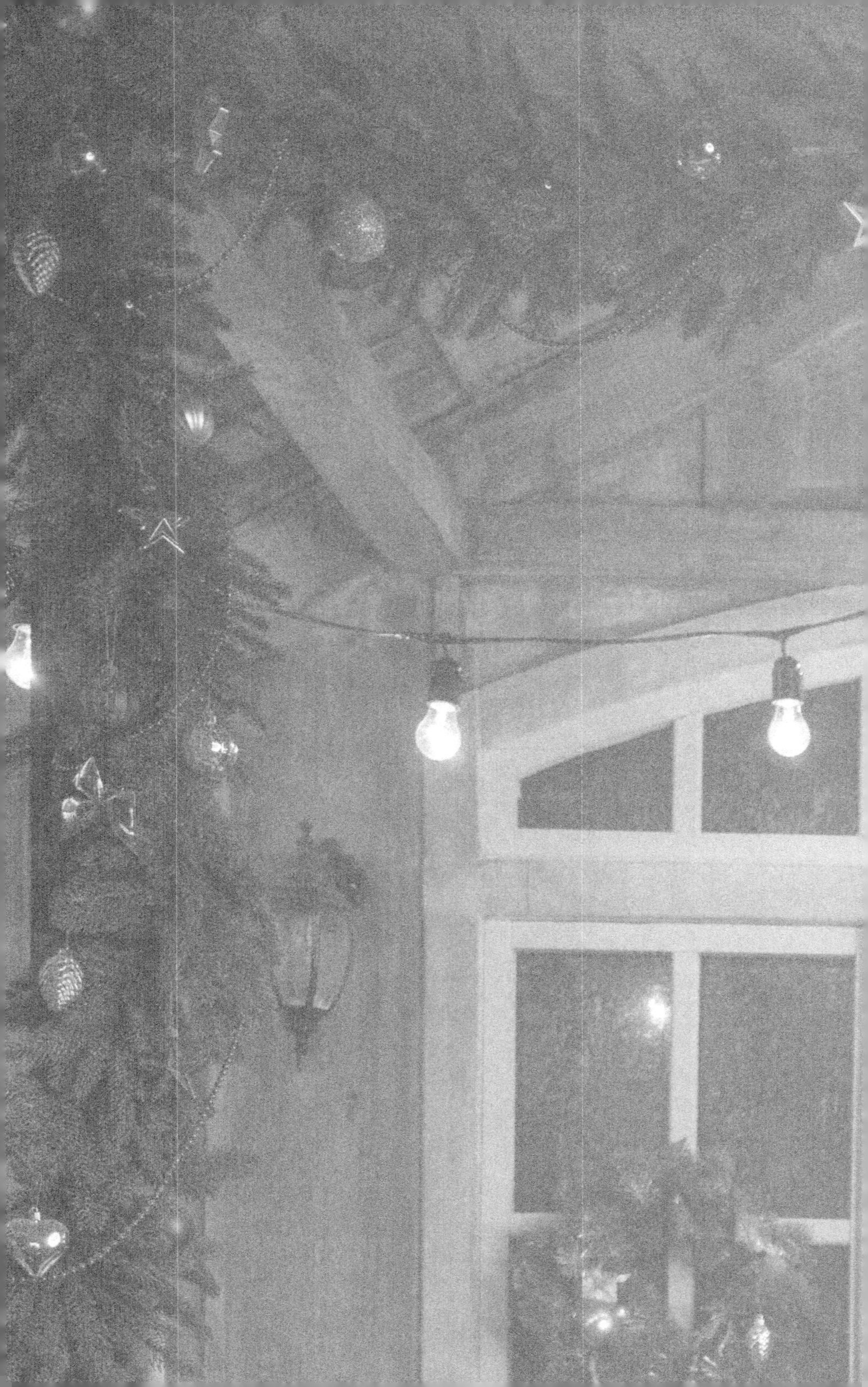

6 / noah

I'M SUCH A CHICKEN. And I'm not sure who I'm more afraid of—Frankie or her brother. Maybe it's a combination of them both.

That was my moment. *The* moment. I didn't kiss her last night, and now I'm never going to get the chance again. I feel it like a rock sitting heavy in my gut.

I blew it.

To top things off, I was basically a zombie at the bar last night, and it felt as though Anthony was grilling me the whole time. First, over the fact I barely finished a single beer. Second, when I didn't lose my shit when the Bears scored a last-second touchdown before halftime. And then when I excused myself early before they pulled off what I'll admit was a huge upset win that everyone will be talking about until the new year.

The only thing I am absolutely sure of is that my old Warrior goalie stick is getting a new home. I simply need to figure out where Conner Graham lives. And find a way to get it out of this locker room without Anthony asking me a dozen questions.

"You want to work the goal a little tomorrow morning?" He swats his hand towel in my direction before flipping open his locker.

"Sure. The sprints are good for me, too, though." I shrug, surprisingly not as winded as I was yesterday. I don't even remember the last set of sprints. Maybe I blacked out.

"Yeah, I know. But I figured even the great Noah Drake could use some practice," he says through laughter. There's an acerbic tone in his voice. I've always sensed a little jealousy, but I try really damn hard to make Anthony feel like my equal. I'm getting a little tired of diminishing myself to make him feel better. Or maybe this feeling comes back to Frankie. Perhaps I'm just tired of him telling me to stay away.

I roll my neck and rub the back of it.

"I've never said I'm too good for practice, dude."

He slumps down on the bench a few feet to my left, tugging his T-shirt and practice jersey over his head before tossing them into the open duffel now at his feet.

"Yeah, I know. I was just fucking around."

I drop my chin and roll my head to the side, forcing a smile I don't mean on my mouth. He's fucking around, but he never finds out. Isn't that how the saying goes?

"You know, I'm sure my sister would sign whatever form you need for school to say you volunteered those hours. I bet we can find other people to take some of the shifts." He stands and grabs his body wash and a clean towel, turning to point a finger at me as he backs away toward the showers.

"I don't like cheating," I say.

He laughs loudly this time, his head falling back as his palm flattens on his stomach.

I scowl, but he ignores my expression and points at me again.

"You're fucking hilarious."

His laughter fills the steam-filled locker area and follows him all the way to the showers as I hunker down for a few minutes and consider his words. Is that really what he thinks of me? That I'm a cheater? Like at hockey? Or . . . life?

I run my towel over my head, drying my damp hair by hand before slipping on a clean undershirt. I'm not planning on being Disco Santa today, though it was kind of fun to catch Frankie looking at me like she wanted me.

I step into the red pants, deciding to wear my compression pants underneath this time. As heavy as this costume is, it's shit at keeping a body warm. Once my outfit is complete, my beard tucked in my pocket, and my gear bag packed, I snag my old hockey stick and speed out of the locker room before Anthony is done with his shower. He's got ten minutes before he has to report to the ice for the kids' camp, so I doubt he'll pay a visit to his sister and me out in Santa's Village.

I tuck the stick on the floor of the back seat of the Bronco just as Frankie pulls up next to me. My pulse quickens, and I feel like a dork for being so excited that she parked right next to me, but I am. It makes it a lot less obvious when I walk her to her car, and maybe I'll find a way to recreate last night's magic.

I'm grabbing my skates from the back when she peers through the window on the passenger side of my SUV.

"Hi," she says, fogging up the glass while she spies at me through binoculars made of her hands. She steps back, leaving two circles in the condensation, then completes the drawing with a dot for the nose and a huge U-shaped smile.

"You're happy this morning." I chuckle. I wasn't happy until now.

"Yeah, I guess I am. Yesterday was fun." She shrugs, then steps around the front of my Bronco to meet me by the driver's side. She taps my chin with a cold fingertip, and I pretend to bite it. I'm relieved when she giggles. I can be playful with her.

"I mean, your beard is missing. There might be kids out here."

"Oh, yeah. Good point." I snatch it from my pocket and loop it around my head and ears, pressing the sticky part under the mustache to my upper lip, but it slips loose right away.

"I'm not sure this thing is going to make it through the season." I blow upward at the fake white hair that's sticking to my lips.

"*Hmm*, come with me."

Frankie tugs the white fluff on my sleeve, and though it's not quite holding hands, it feels a little like it. I let her drag me out to the public ice rink, where she unlocks the side gate for the red carpet that leads to our workshop set.

My eyes scan the rink, and I raise my hand and bellow, "Ho, ho, ho," when a little girl skating with who I guess is her mom pauses to stare at me. She tugs her mom's sleeve, and the woman bends down, nodding before the two of them skate in our direction.

"Sorry, I think I snagged our first customer. Whatever this fix is, I hope you can deploy it quickly."

"I can. Don't worry. You just take a seat on your chair. You can put your skates on there." She literally slaps my ass to send me on my way, and I yelp a little, just loud enough for her. At least, I hope that's all it was.

I scurry to my chair and slip off my slide shoes so I can lace up my skates. Frankie flips open a lockbox and pulls out a small pink bag. She rushes over to me, stopping to greet the little girl and her mom on her way. She instructs them to wait behind the set, shielding us in case this beard business gets tricky.

"He'll be ready in one minute. Santa likes to skate during his breaks, so he's getting his blades on." Frankie sells the story easily, and when the little girl bounces excitedly, I feel as though I want to, too.

"Hold still," she says, unzipping the small bag and pulling out what looks like fake eyelashes.

"Are you going to glue a bunch of those under my nose and hope people don't notice they're brown?" A breathy, slightly nervous laugh slips from my mouth. Frankie leans her weight to one side and pops a hand on her hip as she purses her lips and flutters her eyes at me.

"I'm going to use the glue, bonehead. You get hit a lot with those pucks?"

She pulls the strip of glue from one of the sets of lashes and leans forward, resting her hand on my upper thigh while she steadies her other hand to press the glue in the perfect spot. I'm not sure why she has the fake lashes because hers are already so long and thick. They bat a few times inches from my face until her gaze settles on mine. I don't dare look away, but I can see enough of her mouth to spot the crooked smile pulling up her top lip.

"What?" Her voice is soft but not quite a whisper.

"Nothing. It's just . . . you don't need those things, is all. You've always had really nice lashes."

Yeah, Frankie. I notice your lashes.

My mouth falls into a soft, closed smile as my neck heats. A touch of pink colors Frankie's cheeks. The shade grows deeper as she places another dab of glue above my mouth and fights against letting her smile get bigger.

I lift my hand to position the mustache just right, but Frankie's hands tangle with mine. Our eyes connect.

"Let me do it so it's not crooked," she says.

I give a slight nod, and her delicate fingers press the soft hair against my face, locking it in place. She tugs the beard a few times, then combs her fingers through the curls to give it the official Santa look. Somehow, she has managed to maneuver her body so she's straddling my right leg. My gaze dips, and I shift in the chair, glad I'm wearing both sports boxers and compression pants.

When her fingers sink into the beard and nudge my chin upward, I flit my gaze back to hers. I widen my eyes and relent with a guilty, crooked smile. I expect her to back away and roll her eyes, but instead, she bites her lip, the inside of her leg leaning into the inside of mine in no other way than on purpose.

"How do you know these lashes are real? Maybe I wear fakes all the time."

My head tilts to the side as I take in the entirety of her face.

"They're real. I can tell. I know those lashes, and I know that face."

Her breath hitches, and I feel her air kiss my nose when she exhales.

"You better get ready for this kid. She looks excited," she says as she backs away. I clear my throat as she spins around, and I note the extra sway in her hips. That skirt she's wearing dances just above the curve of her ass.

"She's not the only one excited," I mumble, exhaling with a *whoosh* as I stand and do a lap around Santa's chair.

WE WERE BUSIER today than yesterday. Norris set up just as I finished hearing the *very* long wish list from our first visitor of the day. By the time we finished with the girl's photo session, the line of kids and parents and couples and, awkwardly, random single women, stretched to the parking lot. I barely had time to take a water break, let alone stretch my legs and skate a few laps. I managed to get one session in but was joined by about a dozen kids who wanted to link hands and skate with Santa.

I can't lie. I loved every minute of it.

Frankie and I help Norris pack up again. When we reach his car, he stops us while he fishes something out of his glovebox.

"I figured you two might want to remember this holiday," he says, handing a manila envelope to Frankie.

She eyes him skeptically and slips out a large eight-by-ten photo.

"Oh!" she laughs out, hugging the print against her chest.

"Let me see," I insist, but Frankie only hugs the photo tighter.

"In a minute," she says, flashing me wide eyes.

My body warms and a flash of sweat trickles down the back of my neck as I wonder what exactly Norris captured in that shot. He steps into Frankie, kissing her cheek before speaking something in her ear. His gaze passes me, accompanied by an odd smirk, as he gets into his car.

We both wave goodbye from across the hood of his car. My upper lip still stings from where Frankie ripped the mustache and beard from my skin. I'm not sure I can handle ten more days of that.

"Are you going to tell me what he said?" I finally ask.

Frankie begins to stroll toward her car, and I squint my eyes. I'm pretty sure I've seen this move. When we were kids, she used to swipe the last Otter Pop from my parents' freezer and wander off before Anthony or I noticed.

"Nope." She speeds away, darting for her car a quarter second after refusing to share the picture I'm in with her.

"Oh, no you don't."

I sprint after her, dropping my skates between our two cars as she rushes around them in a figure eight. I finally catch her as she flings open the back door of my Bronco to crawl inside and go out the other side. My arm circles her waist as her hands stretch forward to keep the envelope and photo out of my reach. She freezes instantly, and her arm muscles slacken, allowing me to finally grasp the picture in my hand.

"That's your high school stick. The one you saved for all summer your junior year." Her body flexes underneath mine, both of our lungs working a little extra from running around the cars.

"Uh, yeah," I say, holding my weight up with my free hand grasped around the seat back. Even bracing myself, my chest covers her back.

I lift myself more as she shifts, reaching for the stick on the floor. I sit back on my knees as she moves to lay on her side, holding the blade in her hand.

"I figured I don't use it much anymore. The college bought me a dozen of them, and I'll probably have to use a sponsor brand for the rest of my life, and—"

She lays the stick back on the floor and twists until she's on her back, resting on her elbows while I straddle her legs. This position we're in is so far beyond a simple kiss after getting caught up in the moment. This is the kind of predicament two people fall into before they blur lines for good. I should be reveling in it. I've wanted it for months. I've *really* wanted it for days. But the way Frankie's looking at me right now somehow makes everything feel heavier. It's making me doubt my next move. My next word. Next breath.

"Conner Graham," she says, her voice a raspy whisper.

I chew at my bottom lip and scrunch a shoulder.

"There are two Graham households in Miller Brook, and one is in the senior center, so I figured—"

Frankie sits up in a flash and grabs the back of my neck, pulling my mouth to hers before I have a chance to finish my thought, let alone my sentence. My hands fly to her face, cradling it as her mouth widens to deepen our kiss. A faint whimper escapes her as she breaks for only a breath, then clutches at the buttons along my chest, pulling me down until I'm caging her between my arms.

She nips at my upper lip as I suck in her plump bottom one, my teeth grazing along her soft skin until her mouth eventually slips from my hold. A ragged breath accompanies my name for about a second before she covers her face with both of her hands. I sit up, this time giving her enough room to pull her legs out from under me and sit up on her own, a good two feet of space between us.

I rub the back of my hand along my mouth, not shocked at the smear of pink that comes off. Frankie stares at me with wide eyes, then swivels her head to stare at the quiet and empty rink outside the windshield. She drags her index finger along the edge of her mouth, and I breathe out a laugh.

"You're going to need a mirror."

Her body quakes with a silent laugh, her smile fleeting. She steps out of my Bronco, and I shift to sink back in the seat by myself, groaning when she shuts the door. I'm not sure how many times I'm allowed to get this wrong.

Was that wrong? I let her decide. I followed her lead. That kiss was real.

My brow lifts in surprise when Frankie opens my passenger door and flips down the visor to check her seriously smudged lipstick in the mirror.

"Can I go with you?" Her gaze shifts just enough to meet mine in the reflection.

"Uh, yeah. I'd like that. I mean, I think Conner would like that."

I'd like that. Why can't I just say I'd like that?

I flip over the now crinkled photograph and press the dome light. It's not the shot I was afraid Norris captured, the one where I nearly finished in my Santa trousers thanks to my helper's ass on my swollen cock. But I see what I think got to Frankie. Norris managed to snap the one moment our eyes were locked in a trance, and the strangest sense of wonder and possibility hung in our expressions.

We look like two people in love.

"It's a nice photo."

I smile at it and think of how much my mom would love this shot.

"It is."

I flit my gaze up to meet hers again in the mirror.

"You can keep it," she says.

I drop my attention back to the image, tracing the curve of her leg, light along her arm, and rosy, perfect face.

"Thanks."

She flips the visor back up as I tuck the photo back inside the envelope. I'll flatten it under some books or something. Or maybe I'll see if Norris will print us each new ones. I guess that depends on how this mission goes.

I pull the beard back out of my pocket and slip it on as I climb into the driver's seat. I need to stay in character in case Conner spots me. This job is bigger than me.

"They might lock the gates before I can get you back to your car. You just want to follow me?"

Frankie shakes her head, then reaches her hand to where mine rests on the gear shift. Her palm blankets the back of my hand, and I flex my fingers so she can slip hers in between.

"I'll hitch a ride with Anthony in the morning. I'd like to watch you two skate. It's been a while."

My mouth forms its first easy smile of the night.

"It has."

Four months, six days, and a handful of hours.

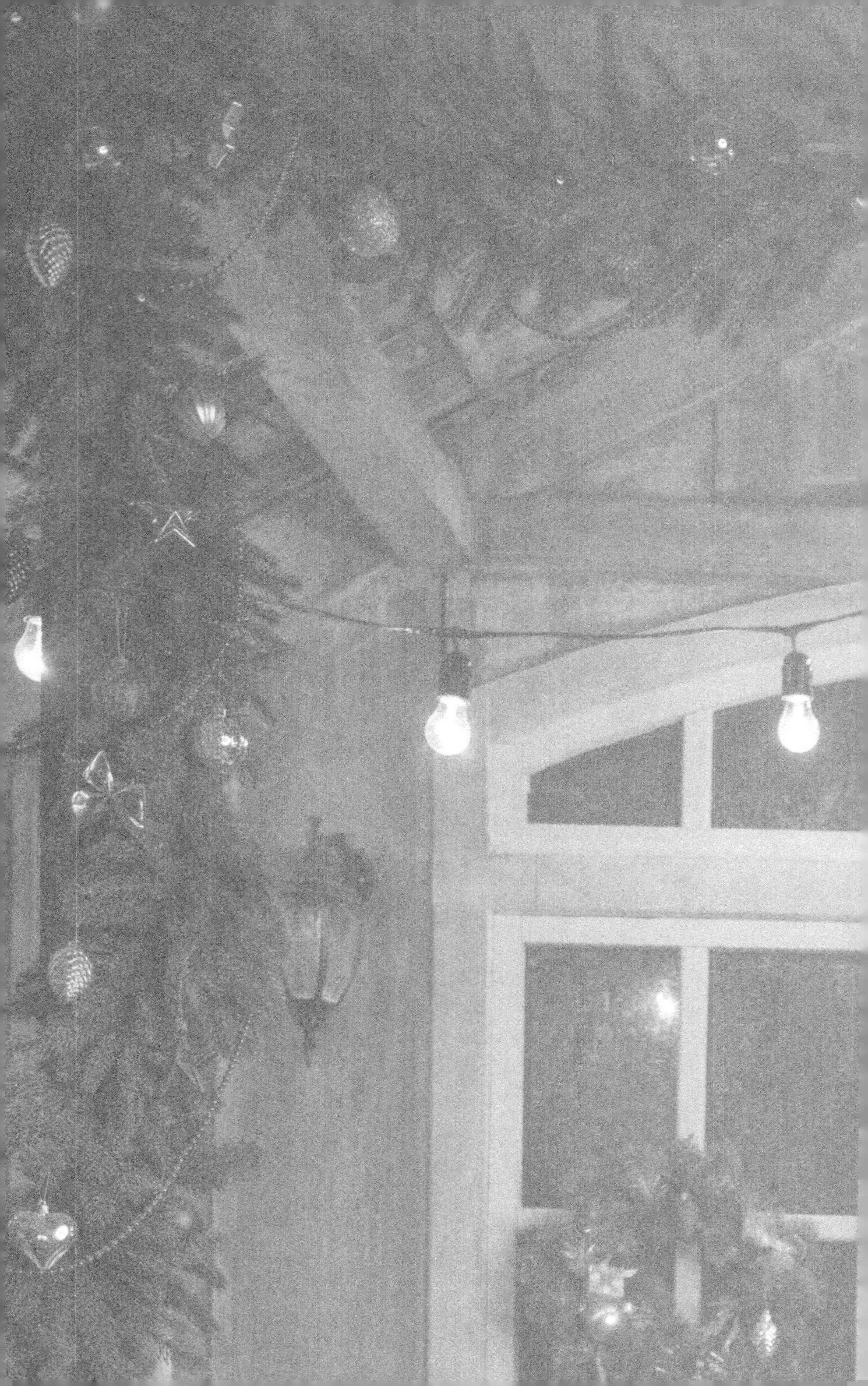

7 / frankie

I DON'T THINK anyone has ever looked at me the way Noah is in this photo.

I've been staring at it the entire trip to what we *hope* is Conner's house. In the moment this photo was captured, I felt something. But I was so swept up in my own swirl of emotions—*should I forgive him, did that first kiss mean anything at all,* and *am I simply overcome with the feel of his body under mine?*

None of that is in this photo, though. All I see is a girl who has been in love with her brother's best friend for years, and a man who might just see her as a woman for the first time.

"Can you tell if that sign says thirty-first?"

I clear my throat and shuffle the photo from my lap, setting it on the envelope on the Bronco's dash before leaning forward and squinting through the frosted windshield. I rub the sleeve of my sweatshirt against the glass to clear the view.

"This is it," I say. Noah makes the turn, then crawls to a stop at the second house on the right.

"You know newer cars come with this function called *defrost*," I tease.

Noah chuckles as he kills the engine, then taps on the switch for defrost just below the driver's side blower.

"They made those in the eighties too. Just not with enough power for Decembers in Illinois." His windows have nearly fogged back up completely in the five seconds we've sat here.

"How's that beard feel?" I unbuckle and shift so I can give it a gentle tug. Noah winces, but the beard stays in place, the glue from earlier still tacky enough.

"I may never grow a real one again if you keep doing that. But I think this one will last for five minutes."

His crooked smile is paired with a wink, and the cuteness of it all pins me to my seat for a moment. I think Noah Drake is the only man I can honestly say looks as good with a beard as he does freshly shaven. And if this costume is any indication, he's going to be one hell of a silver fox.

We both get out of the Bronco. I snag a Sharpie from my backpack before shutting the door, and meet Noah by the rear door as he pulls out the stick. I pull the cap from the marker and hold it out for him to take.

"Here. You need to sign it."

His brow angles.

"As Santa?"

My head tilts, and I pull my mouth in, narrowing my eyes.

"As Noah Drake, dumbass."

His skeptical expression only hardens, so I shake my head and shift the stick in his hand to the flat area near the blade.

"Trust me, Noah Drake means something to that kid. Sign it."

His face relaxes, his mouth hinting at a smile. His hand grazes mine as he takes the pen, and my lips tingle from the memory of our kiss from minutes ago. I brace the stick for him as he forms the prominent N and D of his signature. I almost want to tell him how I practiced signing my name with Drake when I was a freshman in high school.

I dash the urge quickly, though, when the wind picks up. The sun is long gone, and my body quakes from the cold. Noah takes the pen cap from my hand and pushes it back in place, then swings his arm around me, holding me against his warm side as he rubs his palm up and down my shoulder.

"Thanks," I chatter out. As cold as I am, I'm also now on fire from his touch.

He keeps his arm around me as we navigate our way up the bricked walkway. A few of the pavers shift under our weight, and dead grass is matted between many of them. Most of the yard is unkempt. Not junky, but definitely not tended to in months. What was probably overgrown grass and weeds in the late summer and fall is now tangles of straw, and dirt flower beds seem dug up in several spots, possibly from a dog.

"Maybe Santa needs to start a lawn service," Noah

says, scanning the yard on either side as we get closer to the door.

"Santa, or a certain high school hockey team," I say, mostly teasing. Noah, however, reacts with a pensive expression, his lips puckered and brow low in thought.

Before I can question it, we reach the front door. There's a large paper wreath hung around the peephole, cotton balls colored red with some kind of paint stuck haphazardly around the green paper leaves to look like berries. Conner's name is scribbled on one of the leaves. Noah knocks just below it.

His chest expands with a deep breath as his arm slips from my body. Both of his hands clutch the stick as we hover a few feet from the doorway, waiting for someone to answer. Muted chatter grows louder until the deadbolt clicks unlocked, and the door creaks open.

"Oh!" the man says. Noah rests on his heels, as do I. I think we're both relieved we got the right house.

"Mr. Graham?" Noah asks.

"Uh, hi. Santa?" Mr. Graham chuckles, and I cover my mouth with my fist, hiding my own laugh. This is a silly scene, no doubt.

"Babe, who is it?" A slender woman with short brown hair snakes under Mr. Graham's arm. She jolts a touch when she takes in the two of us standing at her door.

"It's Santa, hon," Mr. Graham laughs softly.

"I see that," she says, through a wide smile.

Noah leans in, lifting his beard a little as if either of them really thinks it's Santa. It's sweet.

"Your husband—"

The Goalie and Santa's Little Helper

"I'm John, and this is Sarah," the man says, holding out a hand. Noah shakes it, and then I do the same.

"Nice to meet you, John . . . Sarah. I'm . . ."

"Santa, I know who you are," John says with a wink.

We all laugh softly.

"Yes, well. As I was saying, John brought Conner to visit me yesterday, and your son mentioned he'd really like the new Bauer goalie stick."

Sarah's shoulders drop as she looks up at her husband with a grimace.

"He's been talking about it for months," she says.

"*Mmm*, yeah. It's a pretty cool stick," Noah says. He shifts the one he's been holding, planting the handle on the stoop and spinning it a little to show the scuffs in the light, along with his fresh signature.

"This one is a little different, though. He may need to grow into it, but it's been used in a lot of games, and I've heard that this Noah Drake guy?" He taps on the signature, and I watch for John's expression when he realizes exactly what this stick is. "He's a pretty decent player."

"You're kidding me," John says, cupping his mouth. "This stick is a lot more expensive than the one he wants."

"I am not kidding. Merry Christmas," Noah says, handing the stick to Sarah. She touches it tenderly, her gaze dancing between the rest of us as her husband claps softly. Their youngest is probably inside asleep. Conner may be as well.

"You have no idea what a fan Conner is," John says, shaking Noah's hand again.

My forever crush's cheeks burn a cherry red. I doubt the Grahams can see it. They don't know where to look. As arrogant as Noah deserves to be, he's never been good at receiving actual compliments for his gameplay. The fandom from girls and the hype at Tiff is different. John Graham and his son, and I'm guessing his wife very soon, are *real* fans. Admirers, more appropriately. Hockey lovers who appreciate what makes Noah special.

"Three hundred forty-seven saves last year at Tiff," I brag.

I feel the snap of attention from Noah's gaze as soon as I rattle off his stats. His arm nudges mine, and I glance up at him and shrug.

"I pay attention."

"Noah, seriously. I can't believe this. Are you sure? This is . . ." John weighs the stick in his palms. "It's a lot."

"I'm absolutely positive. It's ready for the next great Miller Brook goalie. In fact, if you have time to take him to the arena by the park tomorrow around eleven, I'll introduce him to the guy running the kids' camp. I bet he can make room for one more."

My face aches from my grin as I make mental notes to make sure my brother follows through on what Noah's about to ask of him.

"Could we get a picture? I mean, with Santa. Maybe with Noah tomorrow," John laughs out.

"Sure," Noah says, shifting closer to me to make room for John to slide in next to him.

"Oh, wait. I'm not much of a North Pole resident in a Bears sweatshirt," I say, slipping my arms out and pulling the sweater over my head. I toss it to the side and shiver as the wind cuts through me.

"Okay, ready?" Sarah holds her phone out and snaps a few shots of the three of us, and then I step out of the frame so she can get a few of Noah and John together.

"I'll print a few of these and put them in a box for Conner to open on Christmas. I'll add a clue for where the hockey stick will be hidden." She's suddenly giddy, and the small injection of joy warms my insides.

My outsides, however? Freezing.

"It was really nice to meet you," I say, rubbing my hands together and snagging my sweatshirt before skipping to the Bronco.

Noah gives Sarah a hug, then shakes John's hand once more before jogging to catch up to me. He opens my door first, holding my hand to hoist me inside, then rushes around to his side to crank the engine and blast the heat.

"That was . . ." I stare with wonder at the fogged-up glass, my mouth open in a permanent smile.

"Amazing," Noah finally finishes.

He leans over the wheel and rubs the windshield with the fur on his sleeve.

"Here," I say, handing him my sweatshirt so he can clear the frost more easily.

When he's able to see the roadway, he shifts into drive and carefully navigates us back to the main highway and over the bridge to the other side of town. He reaches the four-way stop by the small playground before the turn into our neighborhood, but instead of making it, he pulls close to the curb and shifts the

Bronco into park, killing the lights before leaning back in his seat.

His hands grip the top of the steering wheel as he sucks in his bottom lip, eyes blinking methodically as he stares straight ahead.

"What is it?" I wonder if he's having second thoughts about giving away a piece of his story. That stick was important to him, and I know he really wanted to give it to Conner. I'd understand if it stung a little, though.

"You know my saves number from last year?" His head rolls to the side, and our eyes meet.

My tongue peeks out, wetting my bottom lip.

"I do," I say, my voice nearly a whisper.

"You pay attention." His gaze is stuck on mine, and everything feels slow. His nostrils flex with each inhale and exhale. His lips move with what I think are nerves.

"I've always paid attention to you, Noah." The weight of those words isn't lost on me. It sits so heavy in my chest that I shudder with a single sob, but I quickly pull it together.

"I didn't know what to say. This summer, before you left," he continues.

My chest quakes.

"So you didn't say anything?" My voice vibrates. I'm not sure whether I want to leap on him or slap him right now. Maybe both.

He peels the beard away from his face, scratching away the glue remnants as his gaze drops to my mouth.

"Anthony would kill me. I'm not boyfriend material," he utters.

His gaze flits back up to mine. I unbuckle my seat belt and twist to face him. He does the same.

"Anthony doesn't make decisions for me. And he shouldn't make them for you." My lips buzz with desire. The pendulum has swung in favor of lunging at him.

Noah laughs softly, his gaze dropping to the console between us as his mouth curves up higher on one side.

"Funny, you sound like my mom."

My eyes flash wide, only briefly.

"You talked to your mom . . . about . . ." I swallow.

He looks up at me as he rubs his palm on the side of his face.

"She saw us kiss that night in the street."

My cheeks grow warm. Of course she did. I scrunch my eyes shut, then peel one open as I wince.

"She did, huh?"

Noah nods, his gaze dropping to my mouth, then back to my eyes again.

"Your brother thinks I cheat," Noah says.

My brow lowers, and my stomach turns. It's something I've thought about and often overlooked when it comes to my affection for this man. He's had a lot of girlfriends.

I lift my shoulder, shrugging it off, but my movement is tepid. I think Noah senses my trepidation, and he shakes his head.

"I've never cheated on anything, Frankie. Not a test. Not a sport. And never on a girl."

My lungs expand a little, but the knot in my stomach still twists.

"Okay," I say, and honestly, I believe him. There's so

much sincerity in his expression, but more than that, he's being vulnerable. Noah Drake doesn't speak like this. Not to anyone. I would know because I have always been listening.

"I've never actually had a girlfriend. I've dated girls. Gone out. And stuff." He pulls his lips in tight as his shoulder raises. He's a hot college guy. A hockey stud. Kind of a local celebrity. I assume the "and stuff" part.

I've had some "and stuff." But I've never had Noah. And Noah has never had me.

"Okay," I say, twisting in my seat a little more, squaring my shoulders as I scan the space in this front seat and mentally calculate exactly how I can get from here to there.

"You know, I've paid attention to you, too," he says, drawing my gaze back to his.

I bite my bottom lip to quell the shaking. I feel as if my entire body is humming.

"Yeah?"

Noah's gaze trails to my mouth, then lower, pausing at my chest. I drop my chin to see the low cut of my green skating dress, the cut of my cleavage, and then the hard peaks of my breasts poking through the tight fabric. I look back up to catch Noah licking his lips.

"It's cold," I say, moving my hand to my right breast and running my fingers lightly over the hard tip.

"Ha, yeah. Uh, oh-kay." I draw out the syllables as Noah shifts in his seat.

All the times I've studied him, I've never seen him off his game. This feels kind of powerful. I like it.

"It's not *just* the cold, though," I say, bringing my left hand up too and running my fingertips over both my breasts. I pinch my nipples through my dress and the sensation fires throughout my body, pooling between my legs.

Noah lets out a deep, muffled groan behind his fist. His teeth bite at his knuckles.

"Frankie, do not play if you don't want things to go further."

His eyes sear into mine as he inches closer. I shift to my knees and flatten my palms on the console, encroaching on his space. His stare drops to my chest and my tits swell under his stare.

"You wanna hop in that back seat?" I suggest, nodding toward the roomier space.

Noah blinks twice, then flies out the driver's side and into the back seat, sliding to the middle before pulling me through the space between the front seats and onto his lap. I straddle him, sinking down to cover his hard cock and rocking my hips to feel his length under me.

"Holy fucking hell," he moans, dropping his mouth to my throat as my head falls back. His hands glide up my sides and along my ribs, until his palms cover my breasts. He wastes no time taking over what I started, pinching my nipples through my dress and rolling them into tight pebbles. Shocks run through my core and tempt me to come.

"Is there a zipper on this thing?" He feels along my back, finding it quickly and pulling it down my spine until the shoulders of my dress are loose enough to slip out of easily.

I sit up straight and stare at his eyes as they rush with heat. He slides the bodice of my dress over the curve of my shoulders then down my arms, but takes his time to pull it off completely. It's almost as if he's making a show of my tits, torturing himself with the full sight of me bare. Torturing *me*.

When he finally slides the fabric over the hard tips and rolls it down to my waist, my nipples are puckered so tightly I feel as though they might explode. Noah brings his mouth to my right one, pausing with his tongue not quite on my skin. He flits his gaze to me and smirks through the temptation.

"I want to hear you."

I finally let out the gasp I've been holding, and his tongue presses against the hard tip.

"Oh, fuck," I moan, sinking into him and rocking my hips again.

Noah sucks my nipple in as he pushes his pelvis up, grinding into me. His other hand slides along my hip and around my ass, his fingers digging in. I curse these stupid tights. I don't care how cold it is. Why did I wear them?

His fingers scratch at the nylon, the tips teasing at my wet center. I want him to sink inside of me, and my need grows stronger with every touch. His teeth tease my nipple, and he soothes it with a press of his tongue before tilting his head back to look me in the eyes.

"Rip them," I say as my mouth crashes down on his. He meets my needy kiss with roughness of his own, biting my lower lip as his hands claw at the tights over my ass. The material tears for him easily, and his finger pushes inside my soaking wet pussy in seconds.

"Oh, shit," I moan, rolling my hips against his hand. He adds a second finger, pushing in and out at a steady rhythm until I feel myself swollen against his touch.

I scoot back enough to expose the waistband of his pants, and giggle as my hands work the drawstring.

"That's not quite the reaction I was hoping for," Noah says, his breath ragged but tone a little amused.

"It's just . . . I'm about to fuck Santa. That's all." I jerk both the Santa costume and compression pants down his hips as he lifts for me. His cock stands tall and ready, and I wrap my hand around it to feel his warmth and width to ready myself for his size.

His hand touches my chin, coaxing my gaze to his as I stroke him slowly, and when our eyes meet, I know without a doubt he wants me as much as I have ever wanted him.

"You aren't fucking Santa, Frankie. You're fucking Noah Drake."

His eyes smolder as his lips tick up in a devilish grin. His hand covers mine, and he works his shaft with me before holding it up as his other hand guides my body above him.

"I don't have any protection, but I haven't been with anyone since . . ." His ragged voice trails off as our eyes meet. I cup his face in my hands.

Since he kissed me. He's been waiting . . . for me.

"I'm protected. And I trust you," I say, lowering myself

as he tugs my panties to the side, exposing me to his dick. I sink onto his cock slowly, stretching to fit him, and we both moan into the curve of each other's necks.

"Oh fuck, Frankie. You feel so good," he says, pushing up as I sink down.

Our rhythm is slow and steady at first, my hands braced on his shoulders as he grabs my ass and guides me up and down his length. The windows of his Bronco frosted completely, shielding us from anyone who may drive by. The heat is unnecessary now that our bodies are making their own.

Noah's mouth covers mine and I let my hands roam along his arms, appreciating every curve of muscle and familiar scar from the ice. His hips start to lift faster, and my legs widen to take more of him inside me. My knees are so far apart that I'm nearly in the splits as I rock back and forth, chasing the growing need to come.

"Frankie, I'm close," he grunts out. I grab his right hand and guide it to my clit, leaning back enough to let him tease me as his cock slides in and out.

Our gazes lock as we hold our breath, and when he swells inside me, my orgasm ignites, sending waves down my inner thighs and up my belly. Noah pumps into me, filling me with his cum as his thumb rubs wet circles against my clit, drawing my climax out and finishing me with another.

I circle his wrist with both of my hands and bring his hand to my mouth, tasting our sex on his thumb before letting my forehead fall against his. We pant until our breathing slows, and I sit straddling him, his cock still inside, for several minutes as I mentally replay everything that just happened. I can't hide the smile on my face. And I don't want to.

Just when the quiet starts to close in, Noah's palm slaps at my bare ass, and I yelp and laugh. My palms flatten on his chest as I stare into his eyes.

"And what would you like for Christmas, Frankie Bardot?" The flash in his eyes makes me curious, so I rock my hips.

"Again," I say, holding his gaze and holding my breath.

And then his hips rock, and his cock flexes inside of me.

"Such a good girl. I owe you a lot of Christmas gifts."

My eyes roll back at his dominant dirty talk. This good girl really wants to be ruined by this bad boy.

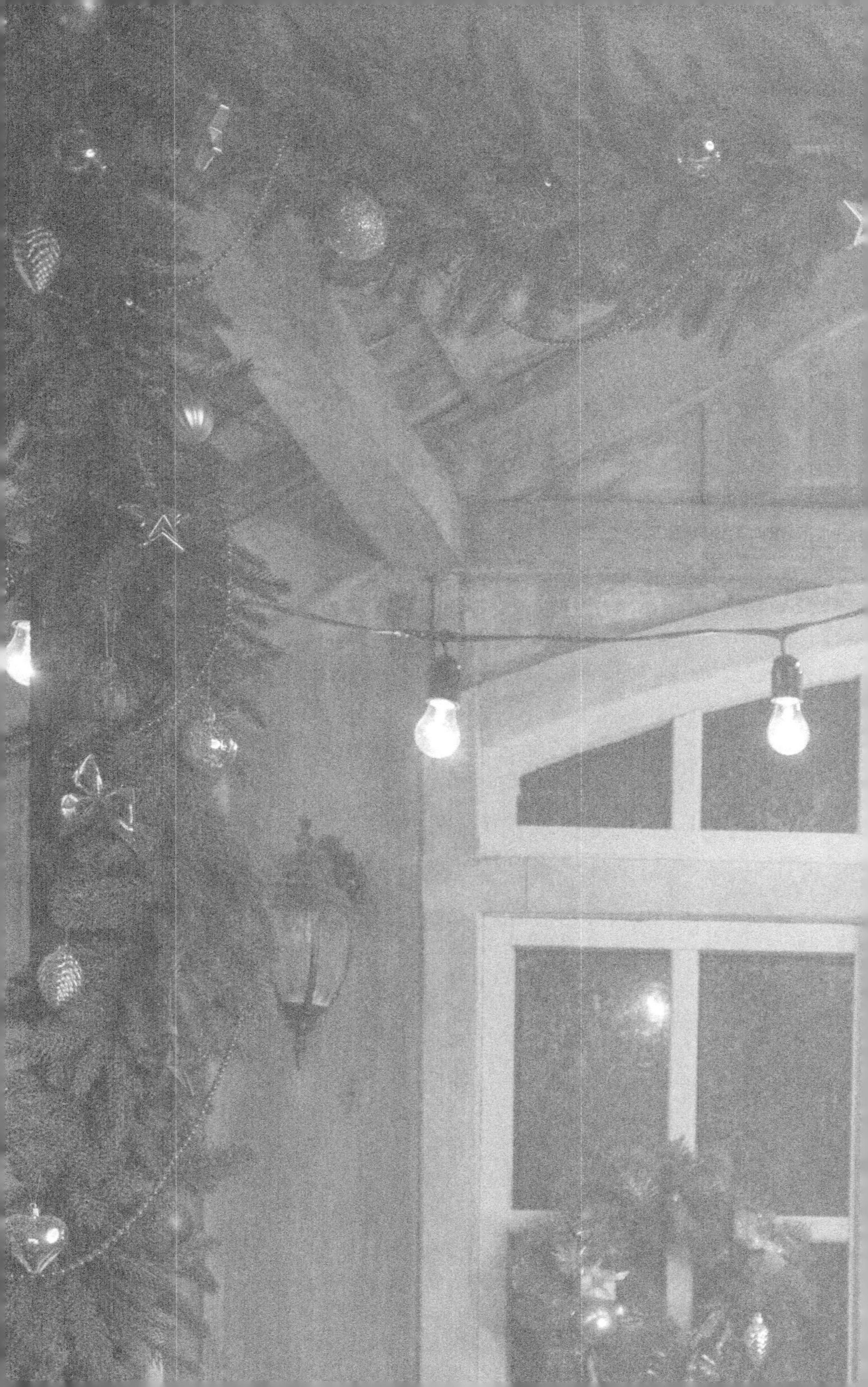

8 /
noah

I CAN'T LOOK Anthony in the eyes. It's making reading his attacks on the rink a little difficult this morning.

For lots of reasons. Mostly, it's the fact I can still taste his sister on my lips. But there's also that shit he said this summer.

You know my sister would do anything to be your girlfriend, right? She's talking about dropping her Harbor State scholarship and going to Tiff. I'm not sure if it's the fact you've been single all summer or what, but maybe be careful what you say to her. I don't want her fucking up her life because of some stupid crush.

It's that *stupid crush* part that hurt. As if her liking me is somehow ridiculous. Don't get me wrong; I admire Anthony for protecting his sister. Sure, he and I always gave Frankie shit growing up, but that's because she's younger and tattled on us all the time. But both of us would have fought off a bear to keep her safe. And then she started high school, guys started paying attention, and we both got protective. Anthony because that's what brothers do. Me, well . . . because I was a petty, jealous fuck who didn't like the idea of her replacing me with anyone else.

Now the thought of any other man having her—touching her, kissing her, holding her damn hand—is off the table. The idea of it makes my blood boil.

But how can I keep her to myself when I don't think I deserve her in the first place? And her brother *definitely* doesn't think I do.

The puck zings by me, nailing the post and flying to the back of the net.

"Shit," I mutter.

Anthony slides to a stop at my side, grabbing the water bottle from the top of the goal.

"What's your deal? Your head isn't in this. That's an easy stop for you, usually. You block that shit with your eyes closed." He tips his head back and squeezes water in his mouth, blinking away sweat as he stares up at the arena lights.

I pull my mask back and rest it on top of my head, taking the bottle from him when he's done.

"I don't know. I think I'm just tired." I spray water in my mouth and swish it around before swallowing, careful not to let my gaze wander to the stands where Frankie has been sitting for the last hour.

She didn't ride with me. We both decided it was better if she hitched a ride with her brother to avoid explaining why she wanted to come with me instead.

Come with me. I mean, that's the reason. It's also why I'm so fucking tired.

When he asked why she left her car here last night, she said Mazy picked her up to hang out. I don't know Mazy that well, but Frankie seemed to think she'd back up her alibi if Anthony went digging. I feel like the house of cards is getting a little tall, and one more lie might send it crashing down.

Those worries seem miniscule, however, when my eyes land on her. She's bundled in sweatpants and a fleece jacket, her hair in braids under the white knit hat with the gold fluffy ball on top. Our eyes meet whenever Anthony's back is turned, like we're in perfect sync. I'm not sure how she's going to handle wearing her costume today unless she plans to keep those sweatpants on. Those tights were unsalvageable.

"Hey, my sister says some kid is coming to camp today, like for free or some shit? You know about that?" Anthony pushes off from the goal, shifting his blades as he slowly backs away, working the puck as he skates.

More cards to add to the house. Conner's dad saw me and my helper last night. Hopefully, the details don't come up.

"Yeah, we had a visitor yesterday. The family's having a real hard time, and the kid eats, sleeps, and breathes hockey. He's a small dude, so just getting to hang with the class will make him feel special."

Anthony nods, but his gaze sticks to me for a few extra seconds, his brow drawn in like he's picking apart my answer in his head.

"You're really in the Christmas spirit, huh? Santa suit getting to you?" He's teasing, but there's something about his tone that feels as though he's asking a whole different question. *Is my sister getting to you?* Maybe I'm just paranoid.

"I guess so. You know me, sucker for hockey fans."

Anthony points at me as he huffs out a laugh, finally turning and skating away. I glance at Frankie, and our gazes connect for a beat. She's chewing at her nails. Mentally, so am I. This is stupid. I should be able to smile at her without worrying about my best friend cutting my legs out on the ice.

For the next thirty minutes, I take shots from Anthony and one of the AHL guys who's in town, and eventually, Frankie leaves to go set up the workshop and meet up with Norris. I skirt out of the locker room just as the first group of campers arrives at the arena. I recognize the Graham's van in the parking, and while I don't *think* Conner would recognize me out of the Santa suit, I don't want to take any chances. After scanning all directions, I sprint to my Bronco, then race to the other end of the parking lot, by the outdoor rink. I change inside my vehicle, and as I'm pulling the velvet pants up under the confines of the steering wheel, Frankie flattens her palms against my window, then cups her eyes to stare inside.

"Oh, shit!" My upper body flails over the console.

Frankie opens my door, her uncontrollable laughter making her eyes water. She leans into the open cab, hugging my left bicep and resting her forehead on my shoulder while I shake my head and pretend to be mad at her.

"I'm sorry," she says.

I sit up but keep her close, chuckling.

"It's fine. I think I'm just on edge. Conner's here for camp, and I feel like your brother knows everything. As in . . . *everything*."

"Aww, I'm so glad Conner came! He's going to have so much fun. And who cares what my brother knows or doesn't know? My life is none of his business."

My mouth forms a tight smile, and Frankie nudges my chin to face her before pressing her lips on mine. Her forehead rests on mine, and she exhales a soft hum.

"You know he would be pissed if he found out. And I get it. He thinks you can do better." I bring my thumb up to her chin, my gaze drifting down the slight space between our bodies. I wish we were alone so I could pull her into the cab and onto my lap.

"What do you think?" she utters after a few long, quiet seconds.

I draw in a long, slow breath and let out an equally long exhale.

"I know you can," I admit. "I meant what I said about not being boyfriend material."

I don't know how to be in a real relationship. I know how to play hockey, be the life of the party, sell the brand of Tiff U Hockey, and make women feel beautiful for the night. But a girlfriend? That's always seemed too serious. But what the hell. Even our team captain, Cutter, has a girlfriend, and he's the least serious dude I know.

Frankie hums, her palm tracing the curve of my shoulder.

"Boyfriends are so high school, Noah. And I think we both know I'm not in high school anymore."

Her hand trails down my chest to my stomach, her fingertips teasing the waistband of my compression pants. The red trousers are still low on my hips, and this simple touch has me hard as fuck. If her hand drops any lower, I'm pulling her into this seat and closing the door so I can do dirty things to her.

"You are definitely all grown up, Frankie Bardot," I breathe out. I shift my body to stave her off, but her hand remains glued to the skin just below my belly button. I let out a nervous chuckle, fighting the urge to shift my cock so it has more room.

"How am I going to get off the naughty list if you keep tempting me like this?"

Her hand slips into my pants, and I suck in a sharp breath as she scans the area around me. I'm trying to be real with her right now. She's different, and I want her to know that. I don't want to screw any of this up, but fucking hell if I don't want to come in her mouth now.

"It's pretty quiet out there," she says, her eyes hazed as her gaze passes mine, then drops to my lap, where her hand has now wrapped around my cock.

My back flattens against my seat as my hands selfishly drift up to rest on the steering wheel, leaving my lap wide open for her to do as she pleases. Goddamn, I hope she wants to suck my dick.

"Norris will be setting up for a while, yeah?" I've only watched his routine twice, but he's pretty methodical. And he's not likely to wander over here to the far corner of the parking lot.

"We don't officially open for forty minutes. And it's

Wednesday." She lifts her shoulder and pulls my cock out as she leans over my lap and rests her elbows on my thigh.

"Yeah, Wednesday. Notorious for nobody going outside," I say, my nervous laugh broken by the feel of her lips on the tip of my cock.

"Oh, fuck. Frankie, I'm not going to take long." My words fall out in a rush. Forget all rationality. This is one of those forbidden fantasies come to life. If I admitted how often I imagined her doing this to me, her brother would definitely put me in the ground. The reality of it is so much better than I dreamt.

"*Mmm*, your dick is warm," she says, her mouth covering half my cock as she closes her lips around my shaft and slides down until I touch the back of her throat.

"Gah!" I let out, my right hand pulling the red Santa hat from her head so I can watch her take all of me in her mouth. I wrap her braids around my fist and gently coax her down my cock again.

"I'm going to come so fucking hard, Frankie. So hard." I run my free hand along her spine, lifting her short skirt as she stands just outside my Bronco. Her cheeks are bare, her legs uncovered thanks to our handiwork from yesterday.

"You are so the naughty one, you know that?" I spank her lightly then gather up the edge of her bloomers in my fist.

"*Mmm*, I am very naughty," she says, her mouth vibrating against my cock as she speaks. Her tongue follows my length as she twists her head to look me in the eyes. Her lips smile against my shaft, and I let go of her hair to push my dick between her lips.

"Take it all," I command.

Her smile remains, and she keeps her eyes on me at first as she slowly fills her mouth with my length. She turns her head again to take me completely, and my palm covers her head. I want to hold her there, to pump my hips. But we aren't in *that* safe of a place right now. Sure, that makes it hotter. It also makes it a little criminal. But fuck, does it feel good.

I lift my hips a little, and she moans. I stare out the window, forcing my eyes to remain open and vigilant, though all I want to do is stare at the ceiling and fuck her mouth so hard and fast. I maintain my discipline but shove her bloomers up higher and run my fingertip along her ass until I find her soaking wet pussy. I dip one finger inside, and she moans as she sucks my cock. It swells in her mouth, and I know I'm going to drown her with my cum in seconds.

"I promise to make it even after work," I say, teasing her while she works me in and out of her mouth. Sucking the tip and pausing for a beat before dropping her mouth down on me again, taking all of me. She grabs the base of my shaft with her hand the closer I get to coming, and when she strokes me while resting my tip against her tongue, I drop my hand on her head. We share a look that I hope lets her know I'm about to come, and she grins against my cock before taking me fully so I can come inside her mouth. She swallows every drop, even running her palm along her bottom lip when she lifts her head and licking away any remnants. It's the fucking hottest thing I've ever experienced in my entire life. And right now, I don't give two shits about keeping a secret from her brother. At this point, if he kills me, I'll just come back as a ghost and haunt Frankie Bardot so I can fuck her every night.

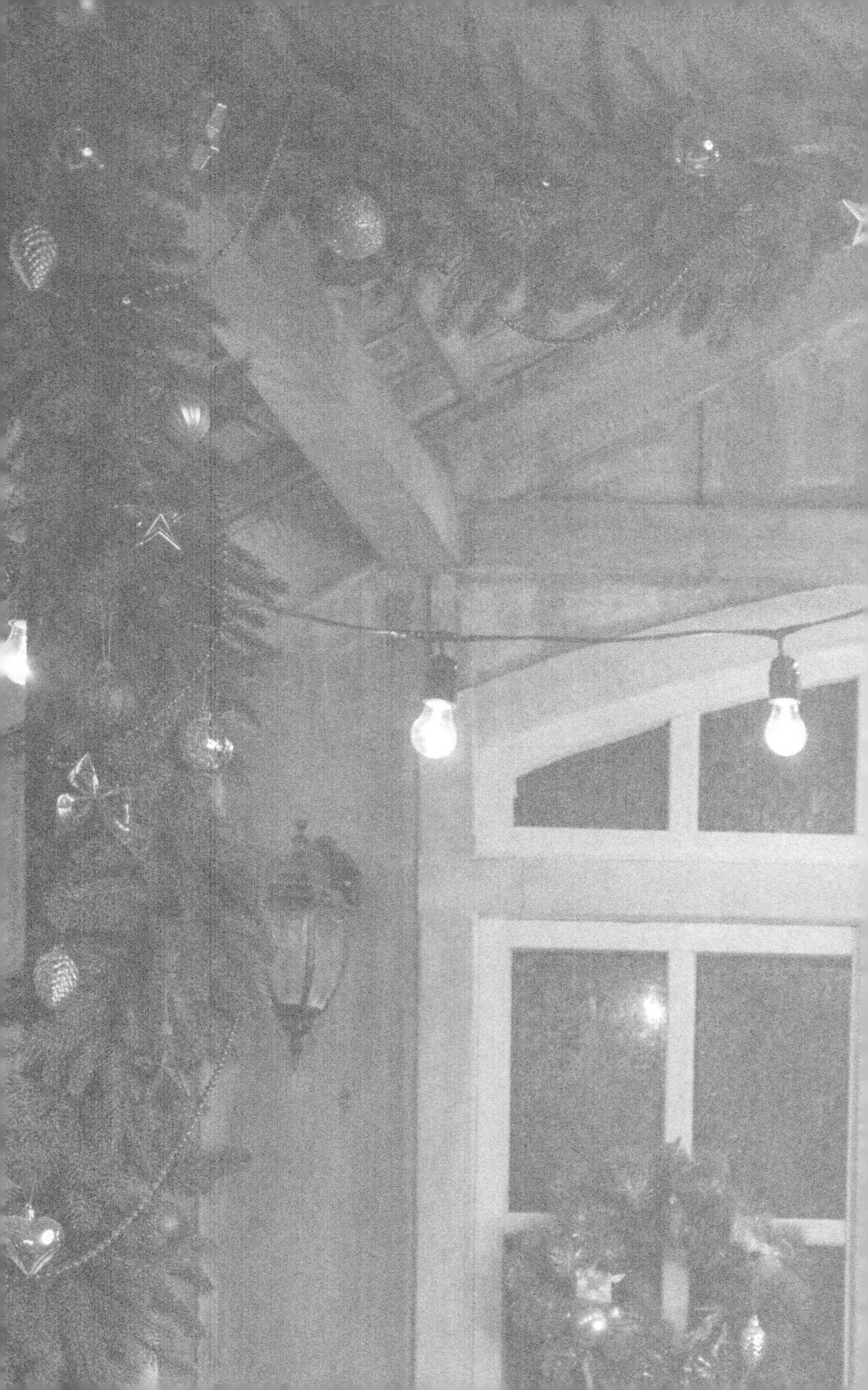

9 / frankie

THE NIGHT of my high school graduation, I had a dream that I snuck into Noah Drake's bedroom and gave him a blow job. I woke up sweaty and embarrassed. But also more curious than ever.

I'm sure it was just my subconscious working through an unrequited crush after seeing Noah sitting next to my brother during my graduation ceremony. Probably a little latent hope that maybe he finally *saw me*, too. He fed me a piece of my cake during my graduation party, and the gesture definitely carried a suggestion with it. Looking back, he was flirting with me then. That was the start of summer. And the flirting continued through the warm summer days at the lake and all the way up to the kiss.

But the clues that Noah saw me as more than his best friend's little sister trace back well before then. I thought about it all night. And as I watched him practice with my brother today, tiny nuances in his behavior jogged my memory more.

During his senior year at Miller Brook, Noah glanced in my direction every time he stopped a goal. Not just sometimes. *Every. Time.*

I didn't let myself think it was special. I was sixteen. He was eighteen. Years that are irrelevant now but felt like the widest valley on Earth just a short while ago.

Then there was my junior year when he and my brother were home from college for the holidays, and I fell asleep outside by the firepit after several of their friends were over to make s'mores and drink cheap beer. They left me out there when everyone went inside to watch a movie or pass out. But Noah? He came back for me. I felt him scoop me up in his arms. I pretended not to wake up as he carried me from the deck through the back sliding door and up the stairs to my bedroom. He pulled my blanket over my body after untying my sneakers and sliding them off my feet. I imagined he kissed my head, and I dreamt so hard that it was real I almost started to believe it was. But I know that part was in my mind. Because now I'm aware of what those lips feel like. And even a kiss to my forehead would imprint on me in a way that left no room for doubt.

And that's why it hurt so much after he ignored me after our summer kiss. I knew I'd never be able to shake it —the memory, the feel, the need for another.

"It was definitely a Wednesday," Noah jokes, referencing my crack about the empty park earlier today as he closes the money envelope after checking my count. We didn't have many visitors today, but the lulls happen every year. I always worry that we aren't going to make enough

The Goalie and Santa's Little Helper

to pay the bill for the community center meal. We always have more than enough.

"You mind depositing the money for me, Frankie? I promised my wife I'd be home in time for the new episode of *The Bachelor*." Norris's mouth stretches with a wry smile, and I'm not sure whether it's because he feels bad that he can't swing by the bank or because he's embarrassed he's hooked on addictive reality television.

"It's totally fine," I say, chuckling. "I can make the deposit in the morning. Enjoy your night. And treat that woman to some deep dish or something. She's a queen, you know?"

Norris salutes me.

"She's a saint, I think you mean." He pats his breast pocket, smooshing his half-empty pack of cigarettes that matches the permanent wrinkles in every shirt he owns. He's one of maybe four people I know who still smoke actual cigarettes. Technically, my uncle Frank—my namesake—smokes cigars. But I'm not sure there's a difference, at least not health-wise.

"What if my Christmas wish is that you finally quit?" My request holds very little weight compared to his wife, Wendy's. She's asked him to quit about a hundred times. He's tried a dozen. And failed every single one of them, miserably.

"Frankie, I think we both know I have nothing to do with your Christmas wish," he says, his gaze flashing to Noah before it returns to me, and he winks.

"Uh," I stammer, my eyes growing wide as my entire body rushes with heat.

"You two are obvious," he laughs out. "But your "secret" is safe with me." He does the air quote thing to really rub it in.

"Not sure what secret you mean, Norris, but thanks," Noah says. I turn to laugh with him, figuring he's trying to put our fling back into the box. But I run into his chest the moment I pivot, and his hands cup my cheeks, tilting my face so he can press his lips on mine in front of someone for the first time ever. Well, other than in front of his mom, but that one doesn't count. And technically, he's still wearing the beard, so I'm really kissing Santa. But . . . semantics.

"Ha, good for you. Have a good night, you two," Norris says, tipping his hat so low it meets his bushy gray eyebrows.

Noah slings the light kit bag over his shoulder and walks Norris to his car. The two of them share a few laughs on the way and shake hands before Norris gets into the driver's seat and backs out of his spot.

"What were you two laughing about," I ask him when he returns. I'm not sure I really want to know.

He gives me a lopsided grin as he closes the lockbox after pulling out my backpack. He still doesn't spill the beans when he turns off the set lights. And I think he plans on keeping his lips zipped as he walks me to my car.

"Noah Drake, if you don't tell me, I am never repeating what I did a few hours ago." I stomp my feet and cross my arms over my chest as I stop several yards away from my car.

Noah laughs out once, then turns to face me, his smirk

only deepening when our eyes meet. He sets my backpack on the sidewalk then steps into me, gently tugging my crossed arms apart and resting my elbows in his palms. My hands flatten on his biceps, and I don't want to feel them, but my fingers curl around the bulged muscles anyway. *Dammit!*

He closes the gap between us, forcing me to look up in his eyes. It's strange how my body still buzzes with nerves as if he hasn't kissed me before. Every time feels like the first. New. Dangerous. A rush.

"Norris told me I better not mess with his girl."

I step back a few inches and tuck my chin in disbelief, and Noah simply nods through soft laughter.

"I'm serious. He thinks of you like a daughter, and he gave me *the talk*. He said if my intentions aren't good, I should hang up the Santa coat, and he'll find a replacement."

"He said that?" My eyes haven't blinked.

Noah nods, his fingers lifting my chin again.

"He also said he's not sure if I'm good enough for you, but he's willing to give me a tryout. Then I think he may have insinuated I was a dumb jock, saying something like, 'You know what a tryout is, right punk?'"

"Okay, now you're making things up," I protest.

But Noah doubles down, shaking his head and stepping back a bit to cross his heart.

"Scout's honor. Or, well, goalie's honor. My honor. Whatever. You know what I mean. And I'm telling the truth."

My mouth hangs open, and I shiver from the cold.

Noah holds up a finger and then snags my backpack, pulling out the pair of sweats from inside. He kneels in front of me as I brace on his shoulders for balance and step one foot at a time into the sweatpants. He slides them up my legs, his hands hugging my hips when they're fully around my waist.

My tongue peeks through my lips, quelling that itch I get every time I want to kiss him. He sways me side-to-side, the air crackling with delicious energy. And then the first flake falls.

"No. Way." I tilt my head to the sky, the dark gray clouds glowing from the city's light pollution as the air fills with more and more specks.

"I told you it was going to snow," he says.

My mouth stretches wide, and I hold out my tongue as the flurries pick up. Noah does the same, but his hands never leave my hips. We sway, our faces waiting to taste more of winter, and despite the lack of music, it's the most perfect dance I've ever had. We giggle, bragging with each flake we catch on our tongues, laughing through kisses that are interrupted by snowflakes that quickly melt against our skin. His beard begins to sparkle, and I shake it out only to watch it collect more flakes.

"I don't know how long the eyelash glue is going to last if it keeps this up," I say.

Noah tugs the side of his mustache, and it peels away.

"Oh!" He quickly presses it back in place, but it doesn't stay.

"Good thing it's late enough for Conner and the other kids to be home in bed." I reach up and press his upper lip with my fingertips, seeing if I have the magic touch. After two failed attempts, I give up. Before I can pull my hand away, however, Noah grabs it with his own, turning my wrist so he can press his mouth against my soft skin as he stares into my eyes.

I'm in trouble. And not the lust-filled kind I've indulged in, but serious, I'm going to open my heart again, trouble. And I'm scared, but I'm going to keep going. Fighting this is no use. It's been years in the making.

"What did you say? To Norris. About your tryout?" I shiver, and not from the cold.

Noah holds my hand against his cheek and tilts his head slightly, his eyes softening and his smile matching.

"I told him I always make the team. And I'm always the best player." His finger strokes the back of my hand as he holds my palm to his face.

I swallow my emotion, my throat so dry in this wet, frozen land.

"Is that what you are? A player? The *best* player?" My meaning is pretty clear. I can tell Noah reads my hidden message by the way his smile falters and his eyes slope. He breathes out through his nose then slowly shakes his head.

"I'm not playing. Not at this. I promise."

I blink rapidly, partly from the snowflakes tickling my face and partly from the tears pricking the corners of my eyes. I'm about to lift on my toes when an engine rumbles in the distance, drawing our attention to the other side of the parking lot near the arena.

My brother's car speeds away. And when I look back at

Noah, his eyes flutter shut, and his mouth forms a silent *fuck*. But Anthony is not in charge of who gets cut in this tryout. And if he saw something, if he says something, if he ruins this . . . I am not only making sure his Christmas is nothing but coal. I'll personally cram it down his throat.

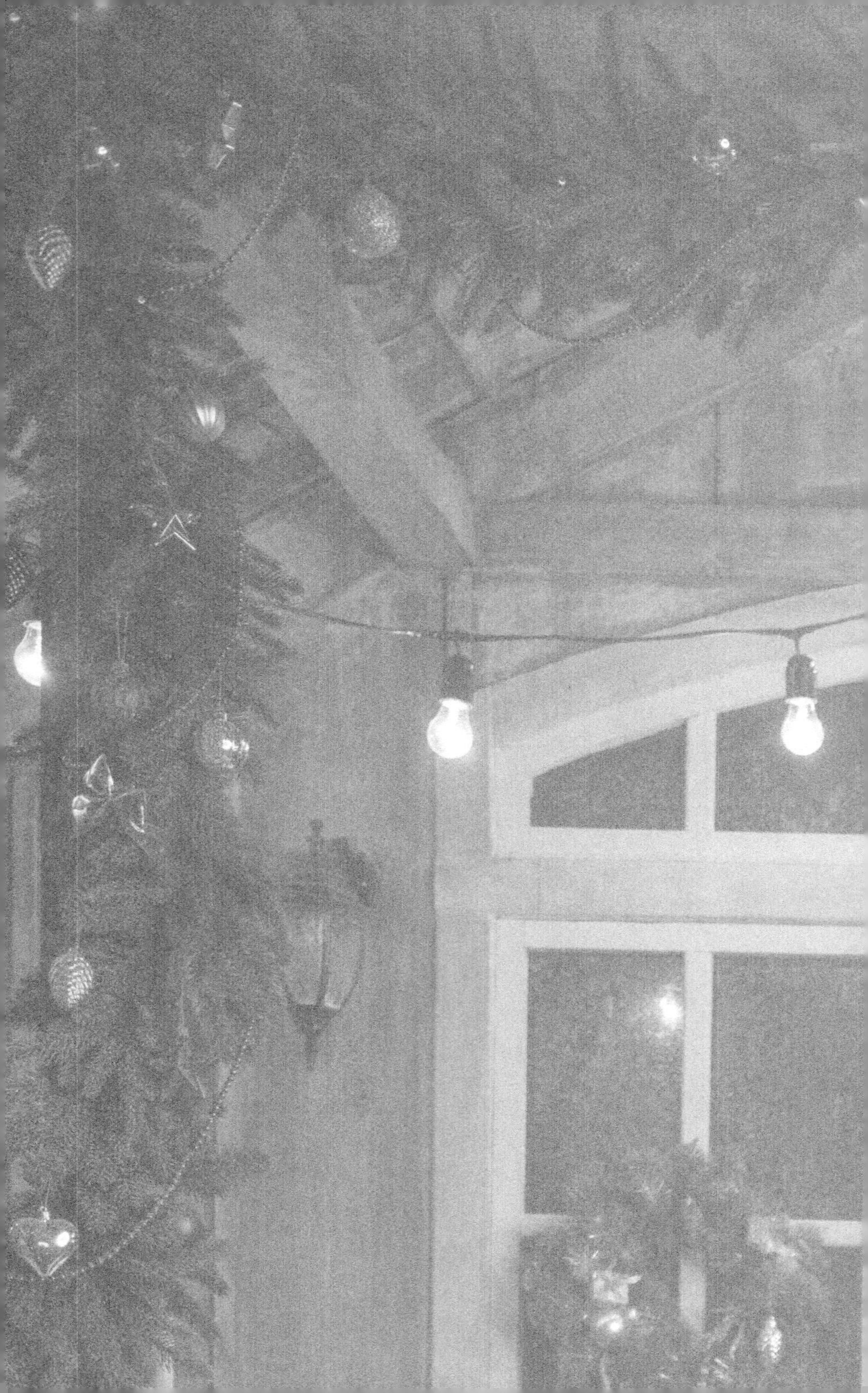

10 / noah

BECAUSE MY MOM is usually the only one in the house, our pantry is awfully full. Even when my dad and I are home, we have too much food on hand.

I've been thinking about that a lot lately. How much we have. How much others need.

Frankie worries we'll be short on covering what the community center buys for the holiday meal. But what about every other day? Miller Brook doesn't have a food bank. Or much of anything else in the realm of assistance. Sure, Chicago is only a little over an hour away, but an hour away feels like a lifetime when you're struggling.

I start to stack some of the staples from our pantry on the counter. Canned vegetables galore in a household that maybe cracks open one can of vegetables a week. Lots of pastas, most of them in sealed packages. Easy-make dinner options. I cooked a lot of this stuff when I was in high school because it was quick and easy, and I could knock it out and eat it between school and practice. But my mom still buys it as if I'm here eating at the same rate. I have a feeling a lot of this gets tossed, and that makes my chest hurt.

"You looking for something, honey?" My mom's shoulder brushes against mine as she peers into the pantry with me. I hold up a can of green beans, check the date on the label, then turn it toward her.

"You planning on eating this soon?"

She bunches her brow, shifting her head to give me a slight sideways look.

"Are you saying you want it? You can have it. It's not exactly breakfast food, but . . . whatever you want."

I sigh and move the can to join the growing pyramid on the counter. I swivel the can of mixed vegetables in my other hand, checking the date. It's the same. Good for another two years. I don't bother asking this time. I move it to the pile and step into the pantry to look for more food.

"I'm sorry, am I not buying the right things? I know tastes change. And usually it's just me, so—"

"That's actually the thing," I interject. I hold up two boxes of the exact same type of pasta. "Do you eat this when Dad and I are gone?"

She studies the front of the box, her eyes narrowing.

"Sometimes. I can make a box, and it will keep as leftovers for a few days."

A box. A few days.

I leave one on the shelf and move the other to the counter.

"Noah, what's this all about?" She steps out of the

tight space in the pantry and leans her back against the fridge. Her expression feels full of concern, eyes dim, mouth tight.

I sigh and lean against the pantry door jamb.

"I gave my high school goalie stick to this kid who came to the Santa workshop the other day. He wanted a new one, not as nice as mine, and I found out that there was no way in hell his parents could afford it. And I don't know, I just started thinking . . . what else can't they afford?"

"Oh. I see," my mom says. Her eyes soften, and her gaze shifts to the stocked shelves in the pantry. I rub my temples, feeling guilty for lots of things, but mostly that we have two of every pasta.

"I know this isn't going to make a difference, but—"

"No, it will." My mom waves off my dismissal. She steps into the pantry and fills her arms with cans, moving them to the counter. She rests her hands on her hips and huffs out a breath, blowing up at her overgrown bangs before our eyes meet.

"Cliché or not, every little action has power. Imagine if nobody stopped to notice or care, and nobody packed up food to share with others who need it? Then nobody would be trying to solve a problem. But you are. And maybe there are a few other people thinking the same thoughts, and what if they see you bring this giant box of food to the photo booth today? They'll think maybe there really *is* something they could do. And maybe they'll tell others. That's how conversations get started. How movements begin. It only takes one person to start something with a chance of getting big."

I scratch at my growing scruff and smile as my cheek presses into my palm.

"I'm one person," I say.

"And now we're two."

My mom steps back into the pantry, gathering more food items. She sends me out to the garage to grab a few of the storage bins that are currently empty because the Christmas decorations are all up. We fill four of them, and I transfer them to the Bronco before heading to the arena.

Anthony's truck was gone well before I left. I'm not sure if he made a stop somewhere along the way or simply headed straight to the arena to get in some extra skating. The one thing I am sure of is that he left early to avoid me. And I left late to avoid him. I don't need to confirm any of it. Some things a person can just feel in their gut—like food poisoning. Friendship betrayal is one of them, too.

The group on the ice is about fifteen strong by the time I suit up and stretch. I jump in for sprints just as Anthony exits the ice, and he goes out of his way to avoid eye contact. We share a house at Tiff. We're teammates. Hell, we're best friends. No matter how awkward this conversation is bound to be, we need to have it. And a day off the ice isn't going to kill me. I'm one of the top five college goalies in the country. My skills will not slip simply because I skip a day of sprints.

I wait just long enough for Anthony to be mid-shower, and I fake a tight quad and exit the ice. I lumber back into the locker room and strip out of my hockey gear, slipping

The Goalie and Santa's Little Helper

my Tiff sweatshirt on along with my black sweatpants. It's early yet. I don't need to be Santa right now.

I wait on the bench between my locker space and Anthony's, and when he finally shuffles out of the showers and spots me, he pauses for a beat, probably running through any alternative exit plan at his disposal. There isn't one. The only way out is by me.

"You got an early start." I figure any conversation must begin somewhere.

"Yeah, you know. Maybe if I put in a little extra when I can, Coach will give me some actual minutes for this year." He flicks open his locker and lets his towel drop to his feet. His very naked body is very close. I scoot back on the bench to give us both some space.

"Why were you so late?" He tilts his head toward the door to the ice just before stepping into his boxers then slipping on a gray long-sleeved shirt. "You hurt or something?"

He sprays deodorant under his arms, wafting the side of his shirt to air it out. His expression is the same as when he's holding a shit hand of cards on poker night. He's playing polite, probably waiting for me to let my guard down so he can take a good swing.

I clutch the sides of the wooden bench I'm straddling and lean back as I weigh my options. Truth? Or partial truth? Do I say I'm tired because I was up late talking with your sister about everything from what she wants to do after college to the fact her brother probably knows we've been hooking up? Or do I totally redirect him?

"We're running short with the fundraiser so I was

thinking about other things we could do to raise money, and next thing I know, I'm clearing out our pantry and starting a food drive."

Redirect it is.

"Food drive, huh?" His mouth bunches, and he squints one eye, kind of like he's examining me for my tells.

I inhale and lift my shoulders.

"I have four plastic tubs in my Bronco, and that's from my house alone."

Anthony nods to himself, continuing to change from his practice clothes into a fresh jersey and sweats so he can work with the kids at camp.

"Why don't we ask some of the AHL guys who are here if they'd do a little charity scrimmage? You can play. I'll play. Some of the high school players. My dad is coming back a few days early. He could play or coach a team. I bet people would pay to play and pay to watch."

It's actually a pretty good idea.

"Your dad's back?" Of course that's what I focus on.

"Yeah. Why? You want him to suit up again? I'm sure he'd be willing to sign off on whatever number of hours you need and take over the rest of the shifts." Anthony closes his locker and leans his shoulder against the door, crossing his arms over his chest as he looks at me. His lips are puckered yet tinged with the slightest smile.

"Unless my sister is growing on you?" Yeah, there's the probing question I was waiting for. Not direct. He's never direct. Anthony Bardot loves to be passive aggressive.

I stand up slowly, weighing all my routes—both

verbally and physically. My insides feel as if I've swallowed a bucket of magnets that are pulling me to the ground. I don't want to argue with him about Frankie right now. Mostly, I don't want him to tell me all his reasons why I need to walk away. I'm not sure I care about his reasons. Especially when they seem to point at how much of an unworthy cheater I am.

"I like this scrimmage idea. Mind if I bring it up to your sister today? I think she's stressed about the fundraiser." I kick my leg over the bench and stand so our shoulders are squared up. I drop my hands in my pockets, making myself defenseless should he boil over and throw a punch. His hazed eyes stare into mine, that gotcha smirk still in place. Finally, he nods.

"Sure. Run it by the boss and see what she says."

I grab my duffel from the ground and sling it over one shoulder, patting my friend on the shoulder with my free hand as I pass him.

"Thanks for the idea."

I pass through the stands at the arena, behind the parents who got there early. I spot Conner lacing up his skates on the other side of the ice, his mom with him today. I hope his dad is back at work. My stress is so petty compared to what they must feel.

I duck out the side door before more kids arrive and anyone spots me and move my Bronco to the same far parking spot as yesterday. Frankie is already at the set, setting up extra lights. She mentioned she was planning to bring a few more strands. She hopes the extra bling will attract more customers. Most of the regulars at the outdoor rink have already ponied up for a photo session. And I'm sure we'll start to get more people out here soon just to visit the photo booth.

She finishes stapling one of the strands along the roofline of the set, carefully stepping down from the small stoop. I realize I held my breath the entire time, not wanting her to slip and fall. I hold up a hand to greet her when she glances my way.

I slip out of the driver's side, a little bummed to see more people at the park today. The snow melted off this morning, so the dog park is bustling with activity. And the hot chocolate stand is finally open. All these things are great for business. Not so great for lifting your girlfriend's skirt.

Whoa. Girlfriend.

I slip out of the Bronco before that thought can freak me out any more than it has in the half-second it took to think it. I slip my sweatpants off and tug the red velvet pants up over my thermal compression pants. I decided to break out the serious layers today. That snowfall last night brought a steady breeze behind it, and it's a good ten degrees colder today.

I work my beard into place using my window reflection as a mirror, then grab the rolling bin from the back of my Bronco. I'd bring all four out to display sample donations, but my mom and I packed several pounds of nonperishables. Frankie will have to work with whatever's in this one with wheels. She meets me at the entry gate as I roll the green and red tub up the sidewalk.

"More lights?" Her eyebrows shoot up near her hairline in excitement.

I pause, my hand on the edge of the lid, and drop my chin as my eyes close.

"Wow, I'm afraid this is going to seem like a big letdown now. I'm afraid it's just . . ."

I pull the lid up, and she peers inside. Her brow scrunches, and she bends down to pick up the box of bowtie pasta.

"Groceries?" She quirks a brow at me.

"Yeah, so after our talk last night, I got to thinking . . . what if we could maybe do more than just raise money? The people who show up for the community dinner probably need some of the basics in their kitchen for the other days too, and—"

I'm cut off by her lips on my mouth and her arms around my neck. My hands fall to her waist as my laughter breaks up our kiss.

"Okay, maybe this wasn't the letdown I worried it would be."

"Noah, this is such a great idea. It's perfect. And you know what? I'm going to call Mazy and have her make us a sign to get more food donations." She flips up her skirt on the side to expose a hidden pocket in her new skin-tinted leggings. She pulls out her phone, then catches my wide-eyed gaze, pausing to laugh.

"You want a pair?" She pulls the fabric out from her thigh, then lets it snap back in place.

"I mean, yeah. Kind of. Women have the coolest things."

She purses her lips, but her smile doesn't totally disappear.

"We have a lot of the shittiest things, too. Don't go thinking a secret pocket makes up for it all." She looks up at me with a hard glare as she drops her chin. I nod.

"Point taken," I say as she swipes to Mazy's contact info and paces down the walkway as she talks to her friend. She sneezes three or four times during her conversation, sniffling by the time she wanders back to me and ends her call.

I give her a sideways look, and she holds up a palm, skirting past me to head toward Norris, who just pulled in with his equipment.

"Don't say a word. I am not getting sick. If we don't acknowledge it, it doesn't happen."

I shake my head and laugh quietly as I trail behind her. "I don't think you can trick germs and viruses like that, but I admire your willpower."

She sneezes again, her back to me, then quickly flashes her middle finger over her shoulder.

"I'm not saying a word," I laugh out.

She sneezes again and spins around.

"You just did. Now zip it." She draws an invisible zipper across my mouth, and I hold up two fingers in Goalie's honor.

When she turns around and sneezes again, I keep my mouth shut. But I also make a mental shopping list for all the things I need for the care package she's going to need me to deliver by morning.

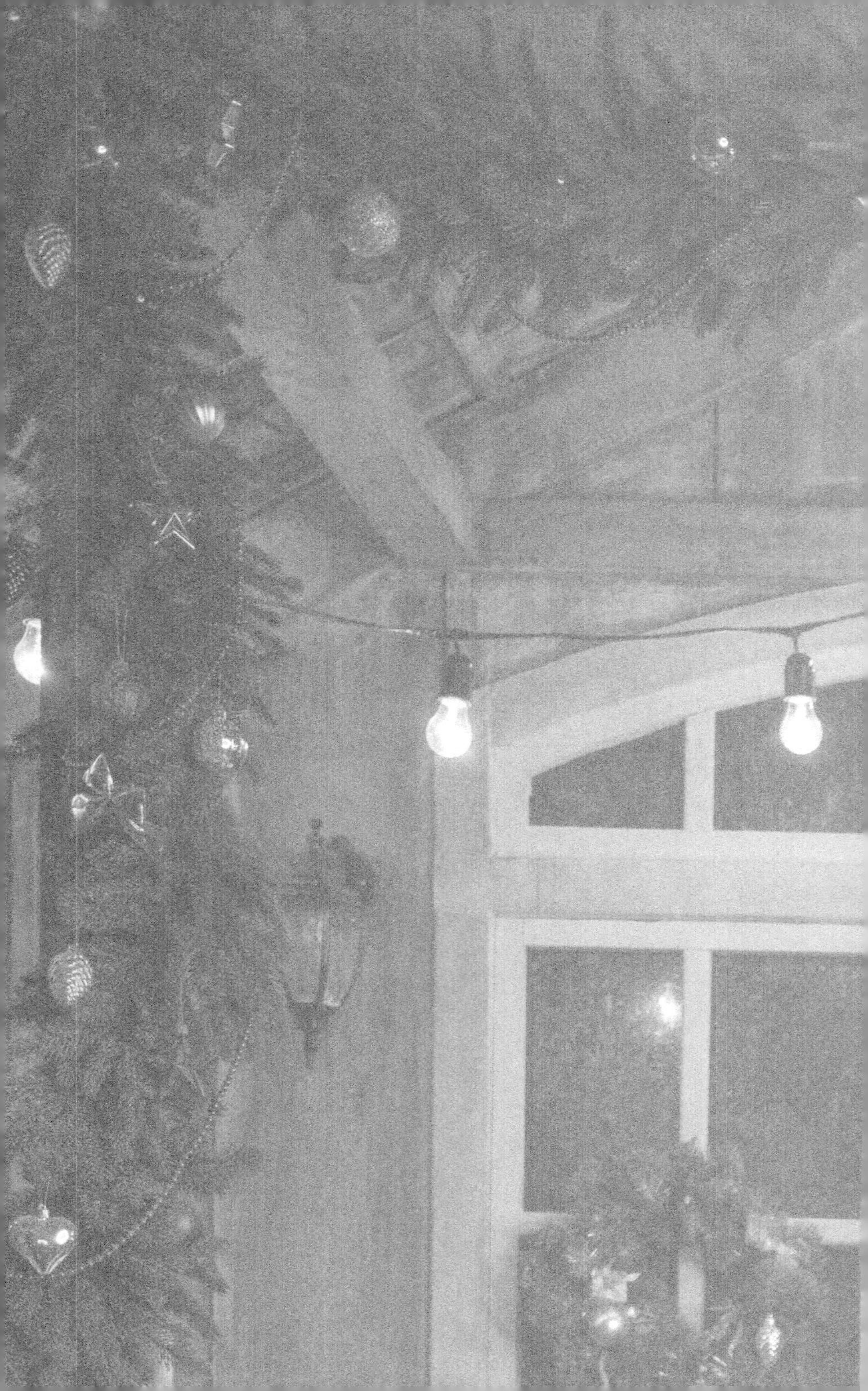

11 / frankie

I DIDN'T REALIZE GETTING a cold was such a great ab workout. I think I'm finally over the sneezing fits, which took up most of my morning and stuck around through the soup and crackers Noah brought over for lunch. I wanted to rally and show up for the photo booth, but Noah insisted I let him handle it.

My dad comes home tomorrow, a few days early, and I miss him. But also, I don't want anything to disrupt the fragile ecosystem of me and Noah and that booth. I'm already hot with jealousy because Mazy filled in for me today. And watching her strip out of my costume in front of me is a wake-up call for exactly how revealing that green outfit is. Noah better have kept his eyes and hands to himself.

"Seriously, Frankie. I know you want to go into social work, but dealing with the public is gross sometimes. I had a kid vomit on my shoes, and at least two older men and one older woman touch my bum. This bum. Right here. Like, my skin is itchy where they copped a feel."

She shivers and makes a gagging sound. I'm less worried about her wanting to encroach on my thing now, and she hasn't mentioned Noah once.

"I should have warned you about the entitled regulars at the rink. Oscar and Milton, the men I think you're talking about? They stopped *accidentally* brushing my ass with their hand when I threatened to do it back with a fist. Georgianne, however? Silver hair and turquoise purse?"

I quirk a brow, and Mazy snaps and points at me.

"Yes, that's the one!"

I nod as she shoves her feet into her leggings and sits on my desk chair to shimmy them up.

"She's a little harder to shake. That's because she's not trying to cop a feel. She's looking for your wallet."

Mazy's head pops up, and her mouth forms an O.

I nod.

"Yeah. She's got a rap sheet, I guess. And technically, she's out on parole. Nobody wants to turn in a woman in her seventies, so she just keeps on rolling with her grift. It's kind of genius. I mean, for theft."

Mazy chuckles, then unzips her crossbody bag and pulls out her wallet to confirm that her cash and cards are still inside.

"How was Noah today?" I finally ask.

She zips her purse back up and lifts her chin, giving me a coy smirk.

"Frankie, staring at that man in a Santa suit all day, made all of the unwanted advances, and apparently mugging attempts, worth it. He is aging so fine. And I didn't realize how big his heart is. I mean, there was a kid who just lost his dog, and Noah spent extra time talking to him about it, showing him pictures of his old dog, which *he still keeps on his phone!* Gah! He's just so—"

"We're hooking up." I cut her off before she professes her love for him because, one, hearing all this is making me so jealous, and two, I am dying to tell someone.

She's frozen, her mouth still half open, ready to finish her sentence, which likely abruptly changed course. I cover my face with my hands and peek through my fingers, and she finally shifts her gaze to me.

"You bitch," she says with a smirk.

"I know!" I force my fingers together again, blocking my view. My friend tugs my hands away after taking a seat on my bed.

"You broke the germ bubble," I say, drawing a circle in the air.

She swats at my hand.

"Frankie, there is no bubble when you have news like this. I'll get sick just to hear the details. I need to know. Tell me everything. Oh, my God, you said hooking up. So that means you've seen . . ."

I nod and cover my face again. She pulls my hands away a second time.

"Big?"

I nod and widen my eyes.

"And how many times?"

I glance up and to the side, literally counting.

"Oh, my God, you have to think about it?"

I giggle and come back to her gaze. "I want to say three, but maybe one doesn't count because I—" I suck in my bottom lip.

"Shut up!" She pushes me, and I fall back into my pillows.

She stares at me as our laughter subsides, but her smile sticks around.

"I'm so jealous, but I know what this means for you. I've always known that Noah is special to you. And you're special to him. I've seen it since high school."

"You have?" My brow pinches. I didn't see it. Not then, at least.

She nods as she gets up from my bed.

"We all saw it. Our friend group? When you weren't around, we called you *that lucky bitch*. But honestly? He's the lucky one."

"Aww," I utter, my eyebrows denting with the sudden need to let my eyes well up with tears.

"Now, I'd love to stick around and eat ice cream and French fries with you like we used to on sick days, but I need to go to my actual job now, the one that gives me money so I can buy Christmas presents . . . for myself."

I laugh at her honesty and hold up heart hands as she blows me a kiss and leaves my room. I check my phone for a text from Noah, but he still hasn't answered to let me know how the day went for him. We got a lot of attention for the food drive yesterday, and Norris got a reporter from our local paper to come out and do a story on it. While I hope that food donations come pouring in, I also hope that the generosity spills over to the photo booth, too. I'm worried we'll have to scale down the holiday meal.

I swish my spoon around the remaining soup in the mug on my nightstand and taste a spoonful to see how cold it's gotten. It's lukewarm, which is too luke for my taste, so I push the mug away, hoping my mom will pass by and take it to the kitchen. It's been a while since I've been sick at home. I forgot how nice it is to be babied.

After nearly an hour of waiting, my phone finally buzzes with a message from Noah. I sit up excitedly, pushing away my comforter and fuzzy blanket as if I'm really going to spring out of bed and hit the town with him. I feel better, but my body feels like it's been run over by a garbage truck. Which is convenient, I guess, since Noah's text says he forgot about plans he made with my brother and a few of their friends to go to the bar and watch the Bulls game.

I pout but send him back a thumbs-up emoji. My phone buzzes again when he quickly sends a heart.

It's such a small, insignificant gesture, but it somehow has my pulse racing in that excited, girl-with-a-crush way. I sink back into my covers and turn off the lamp next to my bed so I can obsess over Noah's social media even more, a thing I've spent most of the day doing. Not that he's ever posted a ton, but there used to be pictures of him with girls on his page. Now, it's just him and the team, or with my brother. And then the shot of us that Norris took. Not all the comments are exactly nice—like the one from Kassie123Me that says the elf looks like a skanky ho. What does she know? I'm not even an elf. But there are a lot of nice ones, too, from both guys and girls. A lot of people saying *cute couple*. And then one from his mom that simply reads: *I told you so.*

I screenshot the photo and a few of my favorite comments. Noah left it captionless, which makes my stomach bubble with curiosity. Is that what we are? Is that our status? Captionless.

I fall asleep, mulling over the thought. When I feel a warm body press against my back hours later in the middle of the night, it takes me a full minute to realize it's not a dream. Noah is here. In my bed. Holding me.

"Hey," I whisper, stretching out my arms and shifting in his embrace so I'm facing him. "Did Anthony let you in?"

His chest vibrates with silent laughter.

"Not exactly. I drove him home. And he left the door wide open, so I figured—"

"You'd let yourself in." I bring a fist to my eyes to rub away the sleepiness.

"I mean, it's not like I could lock up from the outside."

"Very fair," I hum.

"Hey, how's my favorite patient?" He kisses the tip of my nose.

"Careful, I'm probably still contagious." I cover my mouth, but he pulls my hand away and pecks my lips.

"I'm pretty sure I'm well over the contagion line with you."

I breathe out a soft laugh.

"Yeah, I guess you're right."

I nuzzle against his chest, my hand snaking up his shirt

to feel his bare skin. His stomach is so warm, and I swear running my palm over those abs will never get old.

"I brought the deposit over. It was a good day. Double yesterday's amount. And we got a ton of food."

"Mmm, that's because Mazy is a much sexier elf than I am." I tease.

He pushes back and quirks a brow.

"You aren't an elf," he protests. I tighten my lips to hold in my heavy laughter. He has no idea how amusing that comment is right now.

I nod.

"You're right. I know better. North Pole employee."

He smooths my wild hair from my face, his gaze scanning every inch of it. His own is wearing the most adoring expression. Just like in the photo Norris took. It must be a full moon tonight because his profile is lit up.

"No way Mazy is a hotter helper, either. Nobody's hotter. You're the hottest," he says, nipping at my upper lip. The sweet taste of beer lingers on his mouth.

"I hope you're not drunk right now because I like to think you mean it when you say I'm the hottest."

He shakes his head and pushes his hand through my hair, holding the back of my head as our eyes lock.

"I had two beers all night. And I mean it. You are the hottest," he says before leaning in and suckling my bottom lip.

"In fact . . ." His mouth moves against mine, tickling me with his words. "Can I show you how hot?"

I squirm under his spell and let my hand roam lower until I cup his cock.

"So that's a yes?" he says against my ear, pressing his hard-on into my palm.

I nod, shifting so he's under me, and I straddle him at the waist. I flatten both palms on his stomach before slowly pushing his long-sleeved T-shirt up his body. He lifts his head and shoulders to aid me as I pull it free and toss it on my floor. He circles my wrists after my palms flatten against his chest again, every muscle perfection.

I smirk and tilt my head.

"Are you . . . flexing?"

"Absolutely not. This is just how I'm built, baby." His pecs twitch under my touch, and I sling my head back in quiet laughter.

Noah's hands slip to my thighs, inching up my legs and around my ass until he grips both cheeks. He drags me toward him until I'm centered on his cock, and I bite my lip as he releases a quiet groan.

"Have I ever mentioned how great it is that your parents' bedroom is downstairs?" He pushes up against me again.

"Maybe once, when I caught you and Anthony smoking a joint in his room, blowing that shit out the window."

Noah chuckles, squeezing his eyes shut then peeling one open to look at me.

"Fifteen was not my best year," he admits.

I gaze down at his bare chest, trying to remember what he looked like then. At the time, I thought he was so hot that he couldn't possibly be any more handsome. I didn't understand what sexy was.

"You weren't so bad," I say, leaning over him and

letting my hair cascade around my face, shielding us from the rest of the world as my lips brush against his.

"Neither were you," he says, nipping at my upper lip.

I pull back a touch to look him in the eyes.

"You did not see me as anything other than the bratty sister," I protest.

His hands clutch my ass, digging into my skin as he pushes up against me again.

"There was definitely a shift. And it happened a while ago."

I blink slowly, all of my suspicions from before swirling with his admission.

"And now?" I rock my hips as his gaze smolders and trails down the length of my body.

His mouth is a focused, nearly straight line, tinged by a devilish curve as his hands glide to my hips, then up my sides, gathering my cotton nightshirt. I lift my arms over my head as he removes it from my body. He grazes the backs of his hands along my cheeks and jaw as I let my arms fall to my sides. His fingers weave into my hair, combing each side over my shoulder, then twisting the ends in his fingers along the tops of my breasts. Once there, he cups both hands around my swollen mounds and rubs his thumbs over my hard nipples, sending waves of pleasure down to my tummy and core. He pinches the hard tips and holds them tight, pulling me toward him, and I obey, leaning forward a few inches under his command.

His smirk grows.

"Good girl," he says, and I rock against his hard cock again, soaked from two simple words.

His palms leave my breasts, gliding along my ribs as his fingers draw light scratches down my skin until they reach the waistband of my cotton panties. I rise as he pulls my underwear down over my ass and hips, exposing my light strip of hair above my pussy. He leaves me this way, my panties stretched around my thighs, and glides his hands around my ass again, squeezing my cheeks before sliding his palms to the front of my body. He brings his right hand to his mouth, sucking his thumb, then moving it to my swollen clit, gliding along my soft skin before pressing into me.

I arch my back as he sinks his thumb inside me, teasing me with his index finger and holding me still with his other hand. I take every taunt his hand gives me, riding his hand as I sit up tall and move my palms to his waist. I bite my lip to hold in the sounds begging to come out, my body aching for more of him. To feel him.

I grip the band of his joggers and tug them lower, the tip of his cock flat against his stomach, glistening with pre-cum. I rub my thumb over it, and Noah shifts enough to make room for me to pull his cock out completely. He's so hard. So hot. And my pussy throbs with want.

I crawl over his body so I can step out of my panties completely while Noah pushes his pants and boxer briefs down his legs before I return to my new favorite position. Noah guides my hips, lining me up so my pussy rubs against the tip of his dick, and he teases me with it as he grips himself with his hand.

"Fuck me, Noah Drake," I whisper, and his eyes flutter shut for a second, his chest vibrating with a quiet growl.

I lower myself as he guides his cock into me, and I sink down on him slowly, feeling the wonderful stretch and fullness of having him inside me.

"We have all night," Noah says in a hushed voice.

I smirk, loving that I can ruin him so quickly. I'm the one who makes him lose control. It's my body he can't resist.

"Good," I say, lifting up and then sliding back down his shaft. The friction is so sweet, and the way his cock flexes inside of me pushes me to the brink.

I ride his cock with a slow and steady rhythm, my gaze locked on his face, his never drifting from the spot where he enters me. His tongue peeks out as his hips lift, meeting my movement with his own. His hands grip my hips, pulling me down harder with every pump. And I fling my head back as the first wave takes over my pussy and sends tingles down my arms and legs. I'm numb everywhere except where his cock rubs against me, and he keeps pushing in and pulling out, forcing me to take every rush of pleasure that rocks me.

My body wants to go limp, but Noah isn't done with me. And he sits up, sliding his hands around my back and ass so he can shift me to my back as he sits up on his knees and holds my thighs against his hips. With his hands under my legs, he continues to fuck me, licking his lips as he watches my body take every inch of him. I want to see, too, so I lift myself on my elbows. His taut stomach muscles flex with every pump, his fingers dig into my skin, and his cock glistens from my pleasure and soon his own. He pulls out midway and finishes on my swollen pussy, rubbing our cum with the tip of his cock, teasing me with it, and nearly making me come again.

My room smells like sweat and sex, and Noah. His body is covered in a sheen of sweat, and my skin sticks to his as I lay on top of him and focus on the feel of his fingertips as they draw circles on my back. I'm exhausted, and I know he is too. But I want to fuck him again. I don't want to wait for morning. And now that I know the power I hold, I simply bide my time until I can't handle waiting any longer. I grasp him, and he flexes in my hand.

I start things just as before.

"Fuck me, Noah Drake."

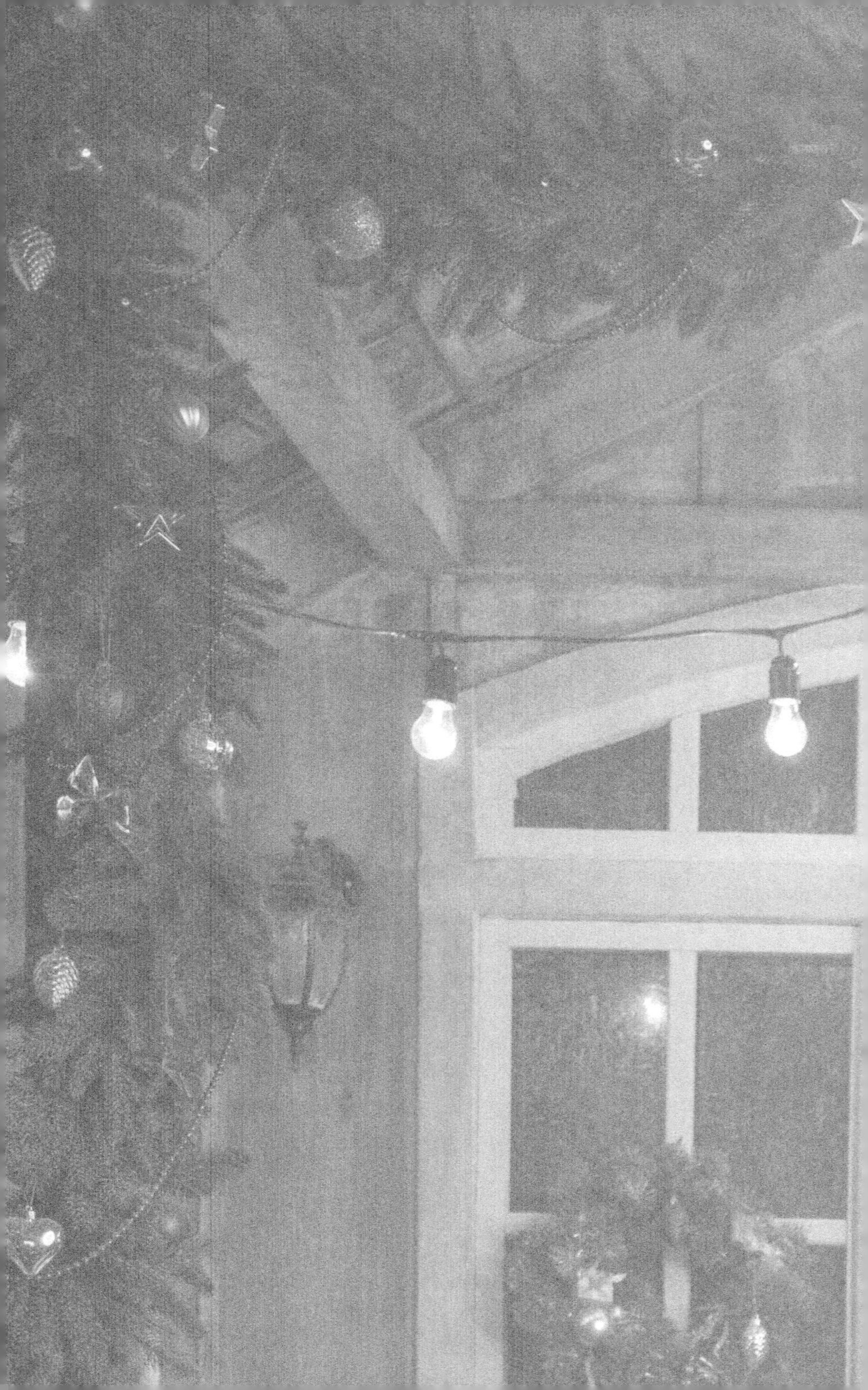

12 / noah

FRANKIE BARDOT OWNS ME.

Completely.

Nothing in my life has ever felt like this. Frankie's body gets me drunk, but her hold on me is so much deeper. She has me thinking bigger. Dreaming more. Seeing a life beyond the draft and what I might do on the ice. She makes me want to put good into the world. And with her at my side, I feel as though I can.

I need to get out of this room before her dad comes home. Before her mom and Anthony wake up. This isn't the way I want her family finding out about us. They deserve to hear the reasons we care about each other. And yeah, Anthony maybe has a right to get up in my face, but his displeasure won't matter to me. I'm not ending my pursuit of his sister. I've held back for too long.

I slip my arm from under Frankie's head, and she stirs, rubbing her eyes and cracking them open to look at me.

"No, don't go," she moans. Her naked body is so hot against mine, but for the last hour, her tits have been growing harder in the cool air. I may have tasted one as she slept, blowing on it just to watch it pucker.

"If I don't get out of here now, the sun will come up and this will be the spot of my death," I joke—*not really joking*.

"Yeah, but—"

She wraps her hand around my cock, which is still hard. It hasn't softened all night.

"Woman, you will be my end," I groan against her lips. I let her stroke me a few times, and I slide my hand between her legs, feeling how slick she is. So ready. So wet.

Mentally, I'm calculating how quickly I can make her come before I must leave. But my brain is thankfully firing enough to know that if we start this again, I'm not going to do anything quickly. I'm going to taste her and tease her. And make her late for the photo booth and cause her family to wonder why she hasn't left her room.

"Fuck, I have to," I say, pulling our lips apart. Her hand slides over the end of my cock, and I twist in her bed, swinging my feet to the floor to give my devil's side some space from temptation.

Running my palm over my face, I smile into my hand as she trails her fingers up my spine, sitting up and pressing her lips to the back of my neck.

"Thank you," she hums.

I chuckle softly.

"For what? Fucking you until you were exhausted or—"

"For everything," she whispers. "For taking care of me when I'm sick, and for running the booth yesterday. And for helping to raise money for our community and being a real Santa to people who need one."

Her hand snakes around my side to my chest, and I bring it up to my lips.

"You make me better," I say.

We sit in the most comfortable silence for several long seconds.

"And thank you for fucking me," she finally says, breaking it up and causing me to laugh a little louder than I want.

"I'll see you in a few hours, yeah? And then maybe tonight you can come with me and my mom to pick out a tree. I think my mom misses the pine scent. My dad usually hauls it home and sets it up, but he won't be home until March."

"Okay," she says, her voice gravelly. Her eyes are barely open when I stand to take her in. I pull my pants from the floor, step into them, and then toss her sleep shirt to her so she can cover up.

"Don't forget the deposit," I remind her, slipping my shirt over my head and stuffing my wallet, keys, and phone into my pocket.

I hold her blanket up so she can crawl back underneath. It's not quite five yet. She still has a few hours of sleep ahead of her. I tuck her in, smoothing her hair from her face before bending down to kiss her head. The mental picture of her soft form will stick with me, and I nearly tell her I love her before I swallow those words so I can process them.

I slip out of her room and gently close her door, not exhaling until I reach the top of the stairs.

What the fuck was that? I love her? I mean . . . shit. I love her.

My pulse races, but with every step I take, it regulates until I'm fucking grinning like an idiot at the bottom of her family's stairs. I grip the round, wooden finial where we used to hang our coats when we were kids after playing in the snow. I glance over my shoulder, up to the quiet, dark hallway beyond the landing, and just before I take a step to rush back upstairs and tell Frankie everything in my heart, a throat clears in the darkness.

Anthony flicks the reading lamp on the second I turn to face the den. He's still wearing the same clothes as he did last night, but he doesn't look as sloppy and drunk. He's sobered up. And he's fucking furious.

"Going somewhere?"

He jumps to his feet and straightens his sweatshirt before adjusting his jeans along his hips.

"Ant, look—"

"You get what you need here? Time to leave?" He takes a few ambling steps forward. I take one back and hold up a hand.

"It's not what you think, man."

"No?" He steps toward me again, closing the gap. He's going to hit me so fucking hard. I brace myself for the impact.

"I really care about her, Anthony. This is different. She's different."

He shoves my chest, two palms dead center, and I lose most of my air and fall back a few steps.

"You're right, Noah. She is different. She's my fucking sister," he shouts, shoving me just as I regain my balance.

"Yes. It's your sister. And I'm sorry that it had to be this way, but I am not backing down." I steady my legs this time, and when he pushes me, I shove him back, my hands hitting his pecs with a massive thud.

"Fuck you," he coughs out, grabbing my shirt by the collar and pulling me into him until the cotton tears.

I wrestle his hand away from me just as his other fist crashes into my jaw. The crunch of bone-on-bone rings in my ears, and the lights overhead illuminate the second Anthony's body rams into mine, knocking me into the dining table, then the floor.

"Anthony! Stop!" Frankie's voice is shrill.

"Boys! Stop it!" Her mom's tone is familiar, the same one she used when we roughhoused as young boys. This fight is different, though. As long as I'm within reach, Anthony is going to keep coming for me. He can't hear reason right now. He doesn't want to.

"I asked you for one thing! One. Thing!" His voice is hoarse from a heavy night of drinking and the volume he's blasting at me.

"You don't get to do that," I grunt, grappling with him as he swings at me wildly, landing a good shot just under my left eye. Eventually, I have him pinned, and I cuff his wrists with my hands and press them into his chest.

"I told you not to fuck up her life, man. She has a good thing going. A scholarship at Harbor. She doesn't need you in her head. You know she's weak when it comes to you. You know it!"

I push his knotted hands into his diaphragm out of anger, and he coughs out a gasp. I'm stronger than he is, even if he's raging. I'm bigger. And if this continues, I'm going to seriously hurt him. As I attempt to climb off his waist, he grabs hold of my leg, tripping me up enough to allow him the upper hand. But I'm done fighting with him. I understand his anger. I just need him to calm down so I can explain.

"I'm going to fucking kill you," he growls, his arm elevated and ready to come down on my face.

"No!" Frankie screams, pulling at the back of her brother's shirt. He fights against her, leaving them both in a strained stalemate as I scoot backward to gain space from Anthony.

He tries to shake Frankie off, and I'm about to leap to my feet to pull her off his back when a pair of massive arms peels her away and wraps around Anthony's waist.

"This stops now!" Steven Bardot's booming voice renders everyone speechless and still. Anthony is not quite limp as his father drags him back several feet, his arms locked around his son's torso and biceps. Anthony doesn't dare fight back.

Still on the floor, I let my back fall against the kitchen cabinet, my mind finally catching up to just how far I traveled during this scuffle. When my gaze lands on the man who coached me as a boy and taught me everything I know about hockey, I suddenly feel like the twelve-year-old who was mesmerized by him. I also feel really fucking ashamed.

"Your eye," Frankie cries, rushing to my side and pressing her cool fingertips to my skin. I gaze at her, my left eye swelling enough that I can see my own cheek puffing up. I wrap my hand around her wrist.

"I'm sorry," I croak.

She shakes her head.

"He made it all up. Did you know that? The volunteer hours? He doesn't need volunteer hours. He was just trying to get in your—"

"Enough!" his father shouts, shoving away from his son and pointing a rigid finger in his face. His dad's jaw is clenched, and now Anthony looks like a little boy, too.

"In your room!" Mr. Bardot growls, pointing up the stairs. Anthony blinks at him defiantly until his dad jerks him toward the steps by his sleeve. "I don't give a shit if you're an adult. This is our house, and you will *not* act like an animal in it. Go!"

His dad points up the stairs, and Anthony scales the steps with heavy stomps of his feet. His gaze sticks to mine, his eyes hazed with a resentment I'm not sure I'll be able to overcome. I let him win, and look away.

"Noah, are you all right?" their mom asks, handing a cloth filled with ice to her daughter. Frankie presses it to my eye, and I wince.

"I'll be fine. I'm really sorry. This is all my fault—"

"Nonsense. You two don't owe Anthony anything. And none of us are blind," she says. My gaze flits to Mrs.

Bardot, and Frankie glances at her mom, too. With a soft smile, her mom squeezes my shoulder and winks, then turns her attention to her husband, who is pacing at the bottom of the stairs.

"I ruined Christmas," I mutter, taking over the cold compress. Anthony's aim is a little too perfect. My face hurts.

"Stop it. You only ruined part of it," she teases. I laugh, then wince.

"Oh, sorry," she says, lifting my shirt to check the state of my ribs.

I cover her hand with mine.

"I can take a check to the body. And this . . ." I circle my face with my hand. "Not my first fight."

She runs her hand through my hair and laughs softly.

"You hockey players are idiots."

I nod and press the ice to my lip, hissing. *Yep. That hurts too.*

"You're not wrong," I agree.

Frankie leaves me sitting as she wets a second towel under the faucet and returns to dab lightly on my face. The pink on the towel isn't as crimson as I expected. I'm going to have some scratches, but I don't think anything is going to need stitches. I think I may have cracked one of Anthony's ribs. I feel like shit over that.

"Santa may need some good makeup today," I say, squinting as our eyes meet.

Her head tilts to the side as she studies me, pressing the wet cloth to my face a few times before her lip ticks up on the side and she grimaces.

"You're going to need a sub today. No amount of makeup will cover this."

"At least the original Santa is home. Maybe it's good that your dad came back early," I say.

She nods, but there's a hint of regret pulling down the corners of her eyes. I recognize it because I feel it, too. This past week has been the best of my life. I love getting to do good deeds with her. I love hearing from the kids and talking with the families.

"Did you really make up needing volunteer hours?"

Shit. I was hoping she missed that part.

My molars gnash together as I let a tight-lipped, guilty smile push into my cheeks.

"Noah!" Her chastising of me is a bit playful, thank God.

I lift a shoulder and let my hand fall to my lip along with the ice pack.

"I wanted a reason to spend time with you."

"You could have asked."

I chuckle and look down at my lap. She makes it seem so simple, and maybe it is. At the time, though, it was terrifying.

"You intimidate me a little," I say. Her head leans to the side, and I shrug. "You do! I mean, you threw that sweatshirt at me pretty hard. It had *oomph!* I was hurt."

Her laughter is soft and subsides quickly, as does mine. I reach my hand up to her face, and my thumb gently strokes her skin. Her hand covers mine, holding my palm to the side of her face, then turning into me to press her lips on the inside of my wrist.

"I won't hurt you again," she hums.

My breath grows heavy. I hold her gaze for several quiet seconds, my heart wanting to say so many things. It's not the time for that. But it is time for a promise.

"I swear I'll never hurt you again either."

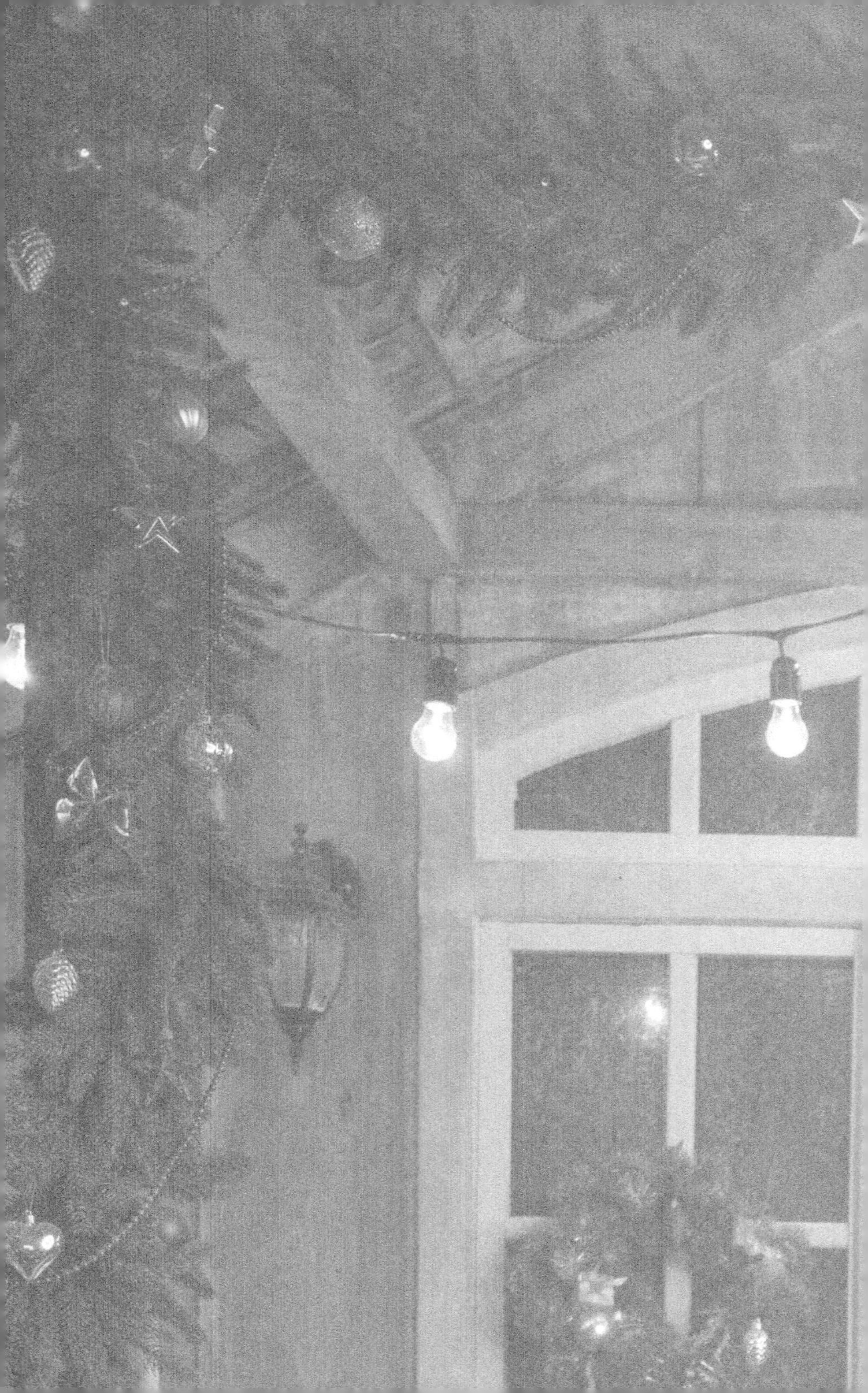

13 / frankie

MY KNOCK on the Drake's front door is timid. Part of me doesn't want them to hear me outside. Inviting my brother to join us as we pick out a Christmas tree was Noah's idea. And it was mature and thoughtful.

But I'm dreading the next two hours. And I don't think Anthony's excited about things either.

"It was a dick move for him to ask Dad like that," my brother grumps.

I smirk, since my back is to him, but utter, "I know." *Really, though? It was smart.* Noah asked our dad if he would be willing to encourage my brother to join us tonight. While my dad took over the Santa suit duties, Noah still came to work the food drive. It picked up steam today and we had a lot more donations.

"Sorry I'm late." Mazy's voice sounds from behind me.

"Right on time," Anthony says. I flash my gaze to him, and he raises his brows.

"Hey, the more people, the merrier, right?" He shrugs.

"What am I missing?" Mazy's attention bounces between me and my brother, and I decide at this point it's best to put everything out in the open.

"Anthony found out about me and Noah, and he refuses to be alone with him so they can talk like adults because . . . ya know. Boys are stupid."

I can sense my brother's glare, so I don't bother looking in his direction to give him any satisfaction.

"Oh, so it's all out in the open now. That's a relief," Mazy sighs, looping her arm through mine.

"You knew?" Anthony steps between us and up the front stoop, but his incredulity is broken when Noah opens the door.

"You're all here. And Mazy. Okay, this might get a little crowded, but we can make it work." Noah steps out of the door, slipping his arms through a puffy jacket.

"Why don't you let my sister sit on your lap," Anthony blurts out. He's being a dick.

"Well, that wouldn't be a very safe way to drive," Noah's mom, Linda, says as she steps through the doorway behind her son. Her lips pucker into a smirk as our eyes meet, and my brother pinches his brow.

"I'm sorry, Mrs. Drake. That wasn't meant for your ears," he says.

"Oh, I know. But you kids were hellions when you were little, so I'm going to live it up now and torture you as much as I can. Consider that one payback for the time you broke my sconce trying to throw a perfect spiral down the hallway." She pats my brother in the center of his chest and continues to pass through us, heading toward the Bronco.

"Classy, Anthony. Real classy," I scold my brother.

"Like you can talk about classy. You're shacking up with Tiff U's Mr. November," he jokes. I get that it's a slam on how many girls Noah hooks up with. And he's trying to make me have second thoughts about him. Except, I've always known who Noah is. I don't judge him for anything. And I believe him when he says he hasn't hooked up with anyone since before summer.

We all trail behind Noah's mom toward the Bronco, but Noah stays behind a step and stops my brother in his steps. They have a brief stare-down, and I hold my breath as I pass them.

"Actually, it was Mr. April. But you're just bitter you didn't make the calendar, so I'll forgive you," Noah finally says.

My brother's head falls to the side, and Noah bites the tip of his tongue, laughing as he backs away. I relax, a little comforted to see them give each other shit like normal.

I help Linda flip up the back seats, and she and I, along with Mazy, climb into the back seat, forcing the two guys to sit in the front together. They don't say a word the entire trip to the tree farm. My brother storms off the second Noah parks, so I hang back in the Bronco as Mazy and Noah's mom exit so he and I have a few seconds alone.

"He'll get over it," I say, reaching between the seats to squeeze his hand.

His eyelashes flicker against the tops of his cheeks as he drops his gaze and runs his thumb over my knuckles. He lifts a shoulder.

"I don't really give a shit what he thinks."

I lean in and touch his chin with my free hand, coaxing him to look up. Our eyes meet.

"Yeah, you do."

His mouth forms a tight, guilty smile. I slip between the seats a little more and press my lips to his, then exit the truck to give him a few seconds alone.

Mazy, Linda, and I weave through the rows of trees, inspecting the remaining inventory. We're a bit last-minute in terms of buying a tree, with Christmas only a week away, but there are still a few beauties on the lot. Their prices, however, come with a bit of sticker shock.

"That's what I get for dragging my feet," she says, examining the tag for the tree she likes best as she chews at the inside of her cheek. Her gaze flits up to mine, then darts to either side before she waves me in closer. Mazy is wandering the rows behind us.

"Don't say anything, but Michael—Noah's dad—he's coming home!" Her whisper feels loud, so when I cover my mouth to hold in my squeal, I glance around to make sure nobody heard.

"He has forty-eight hours, but he really wants to see Noah before the end of his senior season. Maybe pass the puck around. He's going to surprise him on Christmas Eve." She squeezes my hand, and despite how cold it is, her palms are sweaty from nerves. That's a big surprise to plan and hold in.

The Goalie and Santa's Little Helper

"That's amazing! Let me know if I can help," I say.

"Well, I'd ask you to keep Noah distracted, but I think you have that handled." She giggles, and my body flashes with a red-hot blush.

"Noah told me you caught us kissing this summer." I gnaw at my bottom lip, wondering if she's caught us any other times. Like, recently.

"I knew it was just a matter of time. I mean, this is your mother's and my greatest wish," she says.

My mouth hangs open.

"Oh, yeah. We played Cupid. Constantly!" She nods, a rosy pink coloring her cheeks as she smiles. I think she's proud.

"Stop it!" I say in a hushed tone, glancing to my right in search of Noah's head. I saw him leave the Bronco and head in Anthony's direction.

"Every dinner we all had together? Those seating arrangements were strategic. And when your favorite birthday gifts always seemed to be from Noah? We made sure of that. Just, you know . . . nurturing it along."

I chuckle and shake my head.

"I don't know that I'm the one who needed help. I was pretty head over heels from the start."

She waggles her head.

"Maybe, but it never hurts to have your mom helping you shine a little extra. And that dress your mom let you buy for homecoming sophomore year? The one with the—"

"The slit up to my thigh!" I cup my mouth, remembering how shocked I was she spent the money on it and that she let me out of the house in it. Linda's smug grin as she nods fills in so many of the gaps.

"Yep. She sent me a pic from the mall and asked me what I thought, and I knew Noah would die when he saw you in that. And man, you were all he could talk about the morning after the dance."

My wide eyes may never close again. Noah was the homecoming king, and his date was the most popular girl in school. I knew I caught his eye that night, and he even commented on how I needed to watch it because of all the attention I was getting. But I didn't know I made that much of an impression.

"I think you should buy the big one," I say, feeling like everyone deserves a little splurge.

Linda's smile spreads.

"I do, too. Go find the muscle." She pulls the tag and marches to the stand while I hunt down Noah and my brother. I find them arguing in the back corner of the lot, but they zip their lips when they spot me. I wave them toward me, and Noah jogs over while my brother sulks, his hands buried in the front of his hoodie.

"Your mom found one she likes. We'll need to get it on the roof," I explain.

"On it," Noah says, jogging toward the cashier and his mom.

I throw my arm out to clothesline my brother as he starts to pass me, and he huffs but stops his feet.

"What is it?"

He won't look me in the eyes. His best friend looks like a raccoon thanks to the bruises on his face, and

The Goalie and Santa's Little Helper

Anthony is seriously the one feeling self-righteous tonight?

"You are going to get your ass over there and be polite, not for Noah, but for Linda. That woman babysat us. She fed us, and she took us to the fair when we were kids and let us ride the teacups until we threw up. This tree is important to her, and you and your pissy attitude are not going to fuck that up. Now, off you go."

I give him a little push, and though he doesn't move at first, he eventually grumbles his way over to the Drakes to help them wrap and load the tree.

The ride back to our neighborhood feels lighter. At least, it does for me. Noah's mom takes the passenger seat on the trip back, and I sit in the middle in the back between my best friend and my brother. Anthony continues to pout, but I catch him joining a few of our conversations during the ride. He even shares a story about the awesome save Noah made during their last game before the break.

"So, what are your thoughts on the draft, then, Noah? Are the rumors true that Canada may get you out of the gate?" Mazy is simply trying to keep the conversation rolling, but for Anthony, it's one compliment too many. I can feel his temperament shift next to me—his body growing stiff as he clears his throat throughout Noah's response to my friend. Finally, he adjusts in his seat, his eyes on me but his attention on the rearview mirror.

"How's your friend from Thanksgiving, Frankie?" He glances forward, I think trying to gauge Noah's reaction. It's a weird question, and I can't feel the angle out.

"Gus? He's . . . fine." I swivel my head a bit, looking at Anthony sideways.

"Right. Gus. That's *his* name," he says, emphasizing the pronoun. And now everything is clear. Only, my brother is a dimwit, and he has no clue what he's *really* talking about.

"Yes, Gus. I should probably send him a card. Thanks for reminding me." My gaze flits up to the mirror, and I meet Noah's eyes briefly. He doesn't seem fazed. And in a moment, he's going to have a really hard time not feeling smug.

"I'm sure he misses you. I bet he can't wait for you to get back to Harbor. How did you two meet again?" My brother knows basically nothing. This is fun for me now.

"He was my partner for French conversation. He spent some time in France, so I really lucked out with him." I turn my head to hold my brother's stare, and his eyes dim with suspicion.

Yeah, buddy. This is backfiring.

"So, he's . . . French?" Anthony is holding his breath, hoping so hard for this to pan out so he can rub my French friend in Noah's face.

"No, he's American. But he spent time in France. During the war. His wife is an artist from Belgium. They met when he was stationed over there. I think they just celebrated fifty years. When they invited me to stay with them for Thanksgiving, I simply couldn't say no."

I snap my lips closed and let my tight smile rest like a case closed.

"Gus is—"

"A married senior citizen? Yeah. He is."

Noah snorts in the front seat, and my brother smashes his fist against the headrest.

"Shut up," he growls.

Mazy is the next to break. And soon, every single one of us is laughing. Everyone but Anthony, that is. He only shrinks deeper into his seat, and even through unloading the tree and helping to carry it inside, he doesn't say another word.

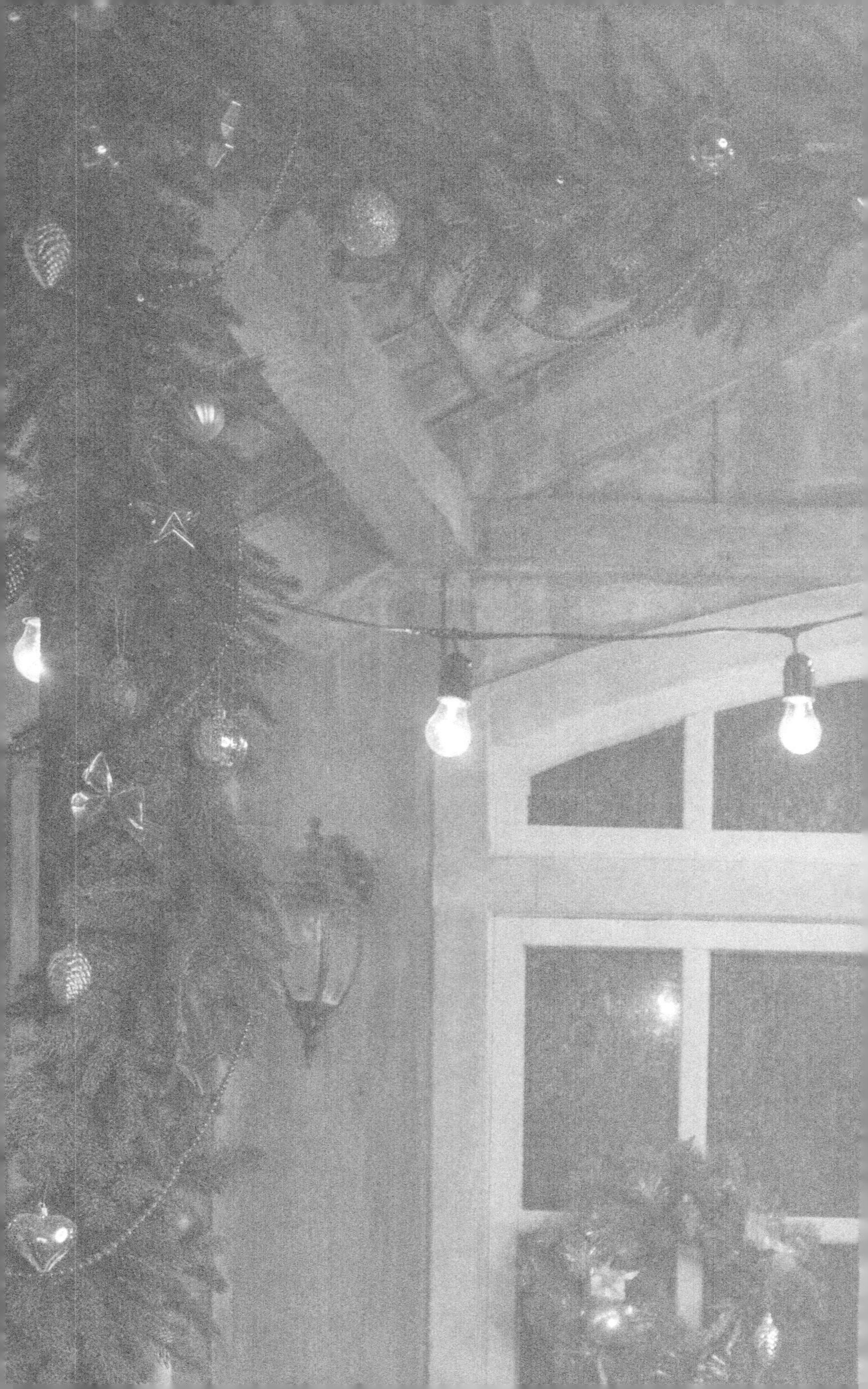

14 / noah

FRANKIE'S DAD really seems to love playing Santa. My eyes cleared up by Tuesday—at least enough for a decent makeup job to cover the yellowed bruises—but I simply didn't have the heart to wrestle the suit from his hands. And now that there are only three days left before Christmas, it only seems right to let the OG himself close out the season.

Honestly, though? I think he's a way better Santa than me anyway. Frankie disagrees, and I don't take her bias lightly because I know how much her dad means to her. To give me the Santa throne over him is a big deal. But I think she's sidetracked by the fact I let her take the Santa jacket off me when we get home. It tips the scales.

Besides, the food drive has been keeping me plenty busy. We passed a thousand pounds in food collected yesterday. I contacted a non-profit that serves our town along with six others within a fifty-mile radius, and they agreed to make nightly pickups. We're going to have food boxes for the night of the community dinner, using a lot of the food we've collected. We should be able to send everyone who attends home with a week's worth of meals.

Whether we can pay the full bill for the meal this year is still Frankie's biggest worry. As pissed as her brother may be at me—at us—he still loves his sister. He loves her enough to put the petty shit to the side for at least two hours tonight so we can play a charity scrimmage with a few of the AHL guys still using our ice.

"Should I coach as Santa?" Mr. Bardot asks me as he stands from the chair and dusts off his pants. He's been candy-caned twice tonight. Somehow, I managed to make it through my tenure without having a single sticky peppermint glued to the suit or beard. I did have a few *other* unfortunate incidents, but I'm blocking those from my memory. All I know is Frankie's mom, Kate, is a miracle worker with cleaning velvet.

"I mean, who can't use a little Christmas magic in their corner? Can I play for Santa's team?"

Really, though, the thought of playing for him again, even something so low-stakes and for fun, gives me a huge thrill. I just need to make sure word doesn't get back to Tiff. They don't like me risking injury.

"Santa it is, then," he says, patting my shoulder with his heavy hand as he moves past me.

I wouldn't say Coach Bardot is as excited about the idea of Frankie and me as a couple as his wife and my mom are, but he's warmer to the idea than Anthony.

I've switched my skating to nights, letting my angry best friend take the mornings to get in his sprints and work out with the other guys. I'm used to working alone. And since Coach Bardot has been home, he's shown up every night to take shots at me. He can only handle maybe an hour on the ice, though. He says his legs aren't quite as conditioned as they once were, so when he's done, I usually do sprints on my own while Frankie times me on her phone.

This scrimmage is all Anthony's handiwork, and I made sure Frankie knew it. He planned the entire thing, and he's the one who had the idea in the first place. I'm not sure why I want her to soften to him so much, especially since his names for me in the past few days have varied from *selfish prick asshole* to *family wrecker*, a term I don't think he fully understands. I guess I don't like the idea of our trio breaking up. And part of the reason I fell in love with Frankie in the first place is because I met her brother first. They need to be whole.

Frankie helps me box up the food for pickup, and I kiss her when her dad's back is turned. He sneers when he catches us touching, again, not because he hates me, but rather, he hates the idea of any punk with his little girl. It's fair. I'm sure one day when I'm a dad, I'll feel the same way if I have a girl.

"You'll be there for the game, right?"

She lifts on her toes to nuzzle her nose against mine.

"Right up on the glass."

I take a mental picture of her excited, rosy face as I back away. I parked by the arena earlier today when I moved my gear to the locker room, so I jog to the arena to dress out and hit the ice a little early.

The locker room is empty, and the arena seems quiet on the other side of the door. I expect to be the only one on the ice when I head down the hallway in my skates. Anthony is the last person I expect and the precise person I want to avoid, at least until we have the comfort of others around to help us avoid talking to one another. But maybe this is the Christmas spirit at work, forcing us together. Alone.

"Hey," I say, getting his attention before skating onto the ice. His head pops up from his stretch, and it's obvious he's been crying. I stare a little longer than I probably should. I can tell he's trying to mask his emotions by the way he suddenly tucks his head and fakes the most ridiculous sounding sneeze I've ever heard. I glide so my back is to him to give him a moment. When he clears his throat, I move to the ice to stretch out my groin.

"I didn't think you'd be so early," he says. His eyes meet mine briefly, the hard line I've grown accustomed to on his mouth back in place.

"Funny, that's what I assumed with you," I say.

A short laugh slips out, and I almost catch a smile on his lips. Anthony is notoriously late to practice. It doesn't help his case for more playing time, but at this point, being late is sort of baked into his personality. His dad has tried to get him to be punctual his entire life. At Tiff, we have a standing joke about him—everyone is told to report at a certain time, and then Anthony gets Ant Time, with an automatic five-minute buffer built in.

"So, how do you want to set this up? Random assignments or team captains pick teams?" I assume he'll want to be a captain. I'm not sure I'd be on his recruitment list today.

"We could both be captains, split up, and maybe work out some aggression?" He quirks a brow, clearly amused by his suggestion. I suspect he's only half being funny.

I fall back to sit on my ass and spread my legs to stretch my hamstrings, mulling over his suggestion.

"You gonna play fair? If you take shots at me?" The thought of him lowering a shoulder and blasting right through me has crossed my mind. I'm running thin on self-control, and my temper on the ice might not stay in check.

"Since when don't I play fair?" He gets to his feet and works his blades on the ice, chuckling as he skates side to side.

"Oh, yeah, that's right. I'm the cheater." My sarcastic tone is thick.

Anthony slides to a hard stop, kicking up enough ice in my direction to make a point. I bite my tongue and give him a sideways look. *Keep your shit together, Noah.*

"You know you aren't exactly the monogamous type. You like your . . . variety. I've watched you turn on your charm at Patty's. What, is that suddenly going to stop when we go back? It's not like Frankie will be around to monitor you."

I get to my feet, keeping my gaze on the ice as I clear my throat and remind myself where his hostility is coming from. I close the gap between us but make sure we're both out of easy reach. No sucker punches, either way.

"You ever stop to think maybe I really, *really* like your

sister? And maybe this *is* different? Maybe I've felt like this for a long time and just kept shit to myself because I didn't want to hurt my best friend. But man, the thought of not going for it and trying to have something special with someone I lo—"

"Don't you dare," he interrupts.

He swivels back a few feet, his chin dropping as his eyes narrow on me, and he points with his glove.

"Those are just words, Noah. You don't get to pretend they are real feelings. Not about her."

I exhale and drop my gloves to the ice before holding out my bare palms.

"Just because you don't want to hear it doesn't mean it isn't real, Ant. I love your sister. And yeah, I've loved her like family for, well, forever. But it changed. It's *been* changing . . . for a while. And this summer—"

"When you fucking crossed the line and kissed her before she was about to leave for college?" he shouts. I figured he knew.

"It wasn't like I had some secret plot, man. We got really close this summer. I spent more time with her, just the two of us, and Frankie and I are a lot alike."

Anthony spits out a laugh.

"Fuck that. She's a social work major who wants to do good things in this world. You're majoring in what? Hotels?"

I roll my neck and tilt my head, pursing my lips at his low insult. He's always been better at school. He's majoring in business, and I wanted something that would be easy to keep my grades up.

"It's hospitality, asshole. But yeah, I agree, okay? Frankie is a better person than me. There, you win this one. Maybe I like that she is. She makes me want to be better. She makes me think about things other than hockey."

"Yeah, well, that's all you're good at, so maybe you should stick with that." His hard stare cuts me, and I hold my breath, the thinnest sliver of control left in my body, keeping me from racing the dozen or so feet between us and slamming his ass into the ice.

"You sure you want us both to be captains, Ant? I mean, you know your dad is going to coach my team and not yours, right?" My eyes harden, but my mouth waters with sudden nausea. That was a low blow, and it hit his rawest nerve. How could it not? Our entire lives, the fact his dad and I had a closer hockey bond than he and his father did has bothered him. Not once, though, did he let that resentment simmer to a boil.

His eyes well up, and he moves toward me slowly. He stops a few feet short and then throws his gloves at my chest.

"Fuck you, Noah."

I catch one of his gloves, unable to look away from his heartbroken expression. I was cruel, but there is something bigger behind this.

He skates toward the boards and flings open the exit, the wood panel crashing against the wall as the hinges overextend. His hand slaps the glass before he heads down the hallway, right back to the locker room, and I remain stunned in place with nothing but my thoughts for the next several minutes. Only when another player enters the ice do I break from my thoughts.

"We aren't starting for an hour, right?" one of the AHL guys asks me.

"Oh, uh. Yeah." I recognize the guy as one of the forwards who came to talk to us at Tiff my freshman year. I should probably introduce myself to him, play the game, and start building the brand in case we end up on the same squad next year.

"I'll be back in a minute. You good?" I start to skate backward, and he nods. I leave my gear on the goal, along with Anthony's gloves, and follow in my friend's footsteps, hoping I gave him enough time but also hoping I didn't give him too much.

I push the locker room door open gently, a few guys laughing as they head my way. I hold the door open wide and nod, repeating what I said to the last guy, that I'll be back in a minute. But when my attention lands on my best friend's back, his shoulders shaking with his head slung forward and clutched in his hands, I realize nothing is going to be resolved in a minute. I might not be back out on that ice at all. Not if Anthony needs me.

His head lifts, and he turns slightly to the side as I approach. He lifts his left hand and waves me away.

"It's fine. Just . . . I'm fine," he croaks.

"No, dude. You're not." I rest my hand on his upper back. He sinks under my touch and then drops his head into his hands again.

I take a seat next to him, leaving my arm around his shoulders, and just like that, we're twelve again, and my best friend is crying on my shoulder—the one place where he can, knowing I won't judge him, and whatever happens here is between us.

"I didn't mean that, what I said about your dad picking me. I was a dick, and I'm sorry."

He nods and coughs out a soft laugh.

"Yeah, that was low, dude. But that . . . that's not it."

I know.

"You wanna talk about it?"

I hold my breath, my stomach twisting the longer his silence stretches on. After nearly a minute he lifts his head, sniffling as he rocks back, and I let my hand fall away. His head swivels until our eyes meet, and his are swollen and red. He shrugs a shoulder.

"My dad's sick, Noah. He doesn't know that I know. Neither does my mom. But I . . . I know he's sick. He wasn't on a golf trip. He was getting a second opinion on his options. I heard him and my mom talking about it over Thanksgiving. And when I heard you call and beg my dad to let you play Santa this year, I talked him into it. I knew he was putting off the second opinion until after the holidays because he didn't want to leave Frankie hanging. And because he loves that fucking red suit, man."

"Ant, I'm so—"

He shakes his head and shifts his weight so he can reach over and hug me. I wrap my arms around him, and he lets out a heavy breath—probably worth the weight of the world—over my shoulder.

"Don't say sorry. I gave you shit for tricking my sister into spending time with you, but really, I made it all happen. And when I found out he was coming home early, I figured it was probably because the news wasn't great."

I peel back but keep my hand on his shoulder. I don't think he needs it there, but I do. I need to hold my friend.

"Does he know that you know?"

He sniffles and nods.

"I told them both I knew what was really going on the night I gave you that." He gestures to my right eye.

I press my fingertips to my upper cheek and chuckle.

"What, this? It was nothing. Barely a flesh wound," I joke, quoting the old Monty Pythons that his dad made us watch a few summers ago. It makes Anthony laugh, which was the point.

"Do you really love her?" His head tilts, and his eyes hold mine, the rage no longer there, but I doubt the worry will ever leave them. And that's okay.

I nod.

"Yeah, man. I really do. And I'm so goddamn afraid to tell her." I laugh nervously. It's so weird to admit this in front of him after everything.

His lip tugs up on one side, and he shakes his head.

"Nah, don't be afraid of that. That's the one thing you don't have to worry about, Noah. Frankie's been practicing writing her name as Frankie Drake since junior high. She's yours. Just promise me—"

"I promise," I cut in. He doesn't have to finish his demand. Whatever it is, I promise.

Don't hurt her.

Love her.

Put her first.

Support her.
Fight for her.
Keep her safe.
All of it. I promise.

"We good, man?" I hold out my hand, and my friend drops his gaze, shaking with a silent chuckle before clasping his hand with mine.

"Yeah, we're good. For now. But we're still both going to be captains. And I'm not planning on taking it easy on you."

I smirk, standing, then helping him to his feet.

"Good. Neither am I."

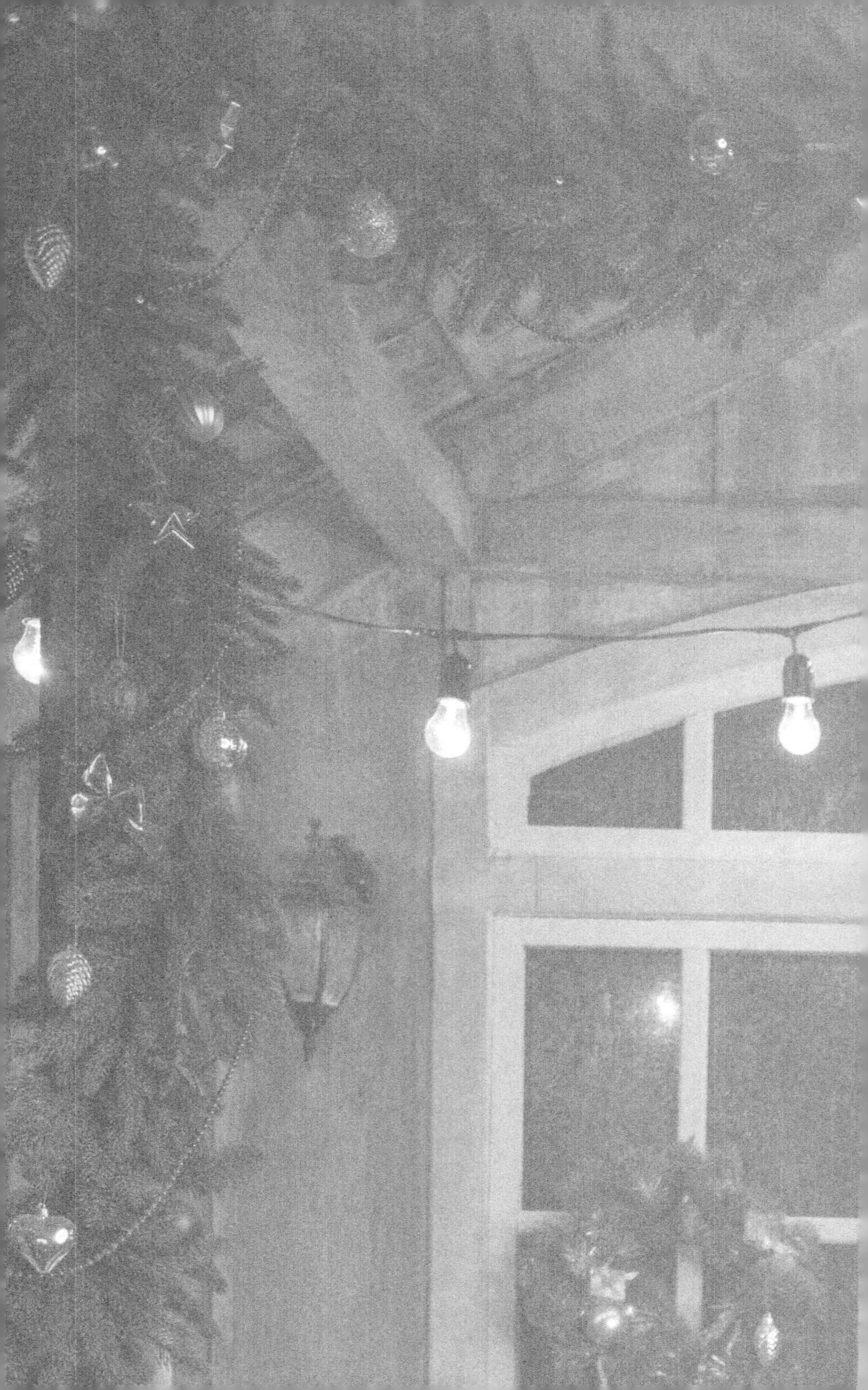

15 / frankie

I'M NOT sure what Christmas magic is happening on that ice, but my brother just scored on Noah, and in return, Noah . . . hugged him. Like, the proud bro-hug thing. Not a passive aggressive "good job, now here's a punch to the gut" kind of hug.

"What is happening?" I utter out loud.

Noah's mom laughs at my side.

"I told him it would just take time. Boys . . . they can solve all their differences with sports." She laughs it off, but I know it must be more. My brother's reaction was more than just overprotective—he was vicious.

To top off the good news happening, the donations we collected at the gate for tonight's game more than made up the difference in what we're short of for the community dinner. There are at least four hundred people here, which for our town on a cold weekday night before Christmas? Yeah, that's a miracle too.

With thirty seconds left in the scrimmage, my brother skates to the bench and holds out his stick for my dad. Dad shakes his head, not wanting to take it at first, but I know enough to know that my father can't turn down a shot at being in a game. He loves hockey. He bleeds it. And after a little—*very little*—goading from the bench, he takes the stick from my brother and enters the ice.

"If he hurts himself, I swear . . ." My mom stands up at my side and loops our arms together.

"Nobody will check him, Mom," I comfort her.

She shrugs, then laughs out, "Yeah, but that man can hurt himself."

True, he's not as agile on his skates as he was a few years ago, but after a few laps, he seems to have found his legs again.

The crowd chants *Coach Coach Coach* as one of the players passes my dad the puck. He maneuvers it around the goal, then moves to center ice as everyone clears out of the way. Noah crouches, and I do not envy this position he's found himself in right now. He misses? He's the joke of the night, the overrated hockey stud. He stops it? He's the guy sleeping with the coach's daughter, who couldn't let up to be nice—not even on Christmas.

"I don't know who to root for," I laugh out.

"Well, I do," my mom says at my side. She unloops our arms and cups her mouth.

"Make him eat that puck, babe!"

I laugh so hard tears prick my eyes. My dad skates toward the goal, and Noah shifts side-to-side, ready as always. I want to cover my eyes, but also, I don't want to miss this. The closer my dad gets, the more serious they both seem, and then out of nowhere, Conner Graham skates onto the ice toward my dad, and the crowd goes even more nuts!

"Oh, no! Trick play!" I shout, cupping my mouth but grinning ear-to-ear behind my palm.

Conner taps his blade against the ice, rushing toward my dad, who passes him the puck, which he misses at first. My dad helps him get control of it, and he stays close as Conner edges his way closer to the goal. Noah lifts just enough to leave space under his legs, and with one quick push—and a little extra muscle from my dad—the new town hero sends the puck through the five hole between Noah's skates and into the back of the net.

The buzzer sounds, and my brother's team breaks the tie, four to three. Noah pulls his mask off and leans on the goal, eyeing Conner as he skates in sloppy circles and holds his stick over his head. It's not *the* stick. Not yet. That comes on Christmas.

My brother skates by and scoops Conner up, hoisting him onto his shoulder while the rest of the players pile around. Noah joins them, kneeling when my brother sets Conner back down, and the two of them bump fists before Conner flings his arms around the man who has my whole entire heart. I wipe the unexpected tears from my eyes and then turn to catch my mom doing the same.

We remain in our seats until the crowd finally clears. Most of the AHL players stuck around to sign autographs and a lot of people asked for photos with Noah. I've never seen the men in my life look so happy and proud.

"Hope the scouts don't get this video," I tease Noah when he finally makes his way off the ice.

He chuckles.

"That kid has a mean push shot, what can I say."

"It was sweet," I say, holding my hand to my chest. He swoops me into his arms and presses his mouth to mine, his hands splayed along my back and circling around me tighter when our kiss breaks, and I fall into his chest for a hug.

"Hey, you okay?" I hum at his ear.

His chin scratches against my neck as he nods.

"Yeah, just . . . that was fun. Ant and I had fun."

I smile over his shoulder and close my eyes, knowing this means as much to him as it does to me.

"You two are always great together, even when you're playing against each other. It was the perfect Christmas show," I say, stepping back when his hold loosens.

His eyes linger on mine, the curve of his mouth not fully a smile, and the dent above his right brow the kind that comes with worry.

"Is he still angry?" I ask.

Noah shakes his head, then bunches his lips, glancing down with thought.

"Well, he's probably still a little angry. But we're good. We worked through things."

I exhale and let my shoulders drop, but the worry on Noah's face is stubborn.

"You're breaking up with me." The words rush out of my mouth like vomit. I might vomit. I can't believe this.

"No, no, no," he says, grasping my biceps and dipping his head to look me in the eyes—which I'm sure are a bit wild right now. My heart is pounding against my breastbone. I feel like a human subwoofer.

"I promise you, Frankie. I am never, like, ever breaking up with you. This?"—he points between his chest and mine—"It's all up to you. You call every shot. I'm not going anywhere unless you make me. And even then, you would probably have to beg me to leave you alone because . . ."

He swallows hard.

"I'm not going anywhere," he says.

I nod nervously.

"Okay," I mutter, moving into his chest so he can hug me again. He holds me to him, my cheek over his heart, his heart drumming as fast as mine.

"Your brother wants to talk to you, and then I think your family has plans. I'm sure my mom wouldn't mind a little one-on-one time putting extra ornaments on the tree. So how about this—when you're done across the street, come on over. I hear you ladies like the Hallmark channel. And we have cocoa.

I eye him skeptically, my pulse still kicking hard.

"Are you sure you don't just want to watch Hallmark? I mean, it's kind of sexist to say it's only for girls," I joke because lightening the mood feels necessary.

Noah rolls his shoulders and puts on an embarrassed

expression, squeezing his eyes shut before popping just one open and holding up his open palm.

"You got me. I'm the one who wants to watch *The Goldendoodle and the Single Dad*."

I laugh because that's genuinely funny. Also, that sounds amazing.

"That better be real," I say to him, tugging on the center of his jersey and pointing for effect.

"I swear it," he says, drawing an X over his chest.

I study his features for one more second before giving in and turning to join my brother. By the time I glance over my shoulder, Noah's back is to me, and he's heading toward the locker room. When my gaze meets my brother's, I'm hit with the same expression Noah just tried to erase from his face. And that's when I know something is really wrong. Something big. I stop a step below where my brother stands.

"What is it?"

His eyes scan the arena, and only a few people are hanging around now, mostly other players and their families. That's when it dawns on me that our parents aren't here. My legs feel weak.

"Whoa," Anthony says, catching me as my knees buckle. I flatten my palms on the bleacher seat as he steps in next to me and helps me sit. He keeps his arm around me. I'm grateful. I have a feeling I'm going to need it.

"It's Dad," he utters after a few long seconds.

My gaze snaps to his. The tears are instant.

"Hey, he's going to be okay," he says, pulling my head toward him and kissing the crown.

I sniffle.

"You promise?"

His pregnant pause makes me quiver, and he squeezes me tighter, then nudges my chin to look him in the eyes again.

"I promise," he says. And while I'm not a thousand percent sure he means it, I can tell by the resolve in his eyes that he will move heaven and earth to keep it. And right now, that's enough.

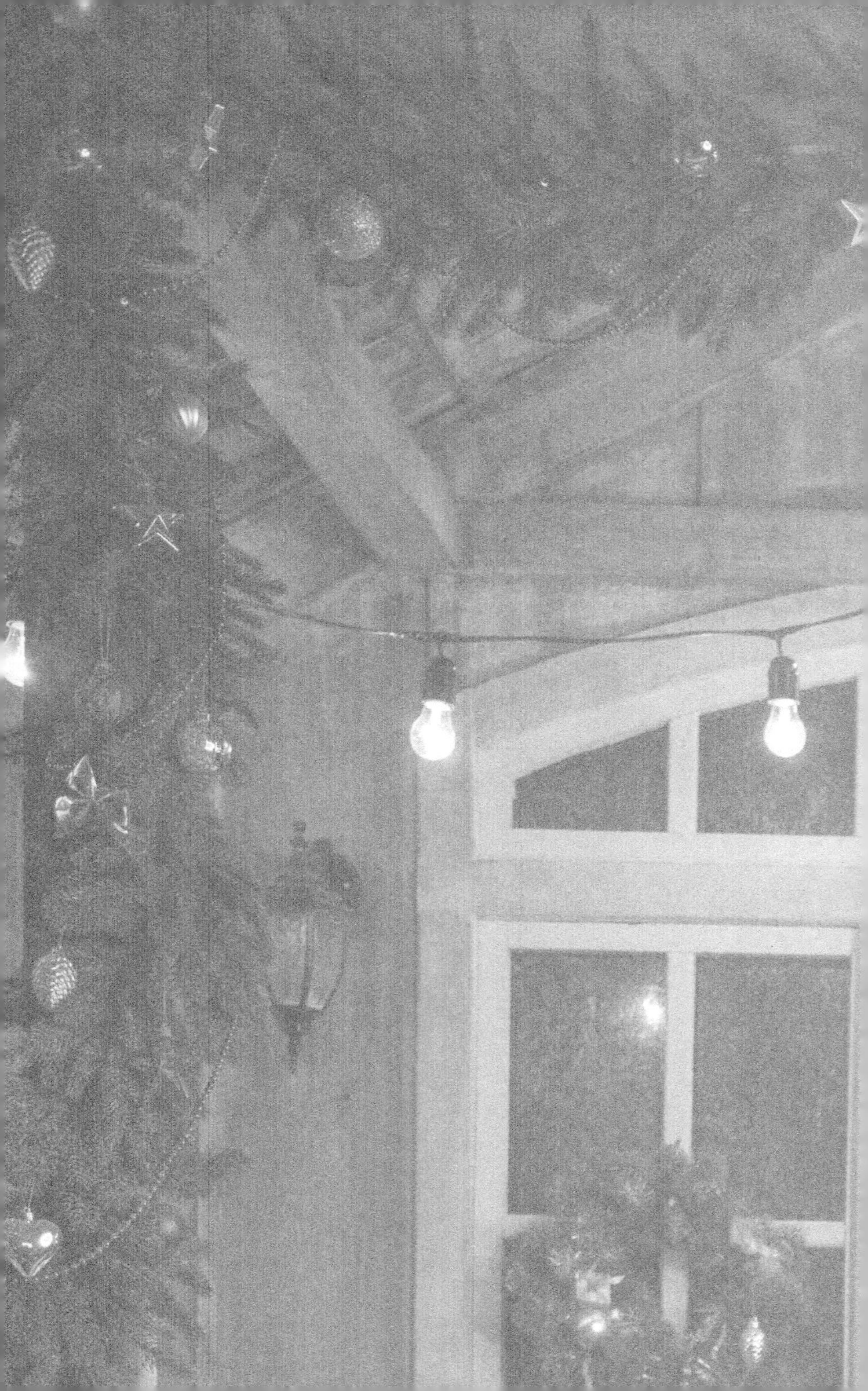

16 / noah

FRANKIE'S DAD has polycystic kidney disease.

It's not terribly uncommon, and it can usually be managed with careful diet, exercise, medication, and dialysis. But not his.

Steven Bardot didn't see it coming. He thought the headaches were part of his job. He's a machinist, and before people started paying attention to things like hearing damage, he didn't exactly follow protocol and wear the right protection. He thought maybe it could have been the effects of years of pick-up hockey, too, or from coaching kids half his life. When he started to get dizzy, his wife made him get answers.

Hypertension seemed obvious enough; he's in his late fifties. And his diet has always relied heavily on drive-thru windows. But then the kidney tests came back. In less than a month, he went from being the stubborn man putting off the doctor to the guy in need of a new kidney.

I filled my mom in on everything Anthony told me, and

I've been waiting on our front stoop for the last hour for Frankie to step outside. It started snowing about ten minutes ago, hard enough to dust the ground between our houses. They'll need to clear the roads by morning. Winter is here.

I pull the knit cap lower on my head, covering my ears, then blow into my hands again before stuffing them into the pockets of my winter coat. The warm glow from the Bardot house across the streets catches my gaze as Frankie opens the door. She's not dressed for this weather, wearing nothing but an oversized shirt and purple unicorn slippers, but she shuts the door and walks in my direction anyhow.

I get to my feet and jog toward her, scooping her into my arms so I can carry her to my warm room. Her head falls into my chest along the way, her eyes red but no longer wet from crying. My door slams shut with my kick, and I lay her down in my bed, pull off my jacket, and slip in beside her under the quilt made of my jerseys.

"You said it was going to snow," she mutters. Her voice seems emotionless.

I stroke her hair and kiss her forehead.

"I did. I kind of cheated, though," I admit.

Her eyes flutter up to meet mine.

"You aren't a cheater," she says, still defending me against her brother's accusation. A tight smile hits my lips, and I slowly blink my appreciation.

"Okay, maybe I didn't *cheat*. I simply used my resources. I have a really nerdy weather app, and my favorite guy who posts on there wrote that the science pointed to snow."

"Ah," she says, her voice and her body listless.

The back of my hand brushes along her cheek, sweeping away a few stray hairs. She reaches up and presses my palm to her face, then nestles into my pillow and stares at me.

"Tell me about your dad," she says.

Her ask surprises me a little. I wasn't sure if she wanted to talk or sleep or watch mindless videos, but I figured it would be one of those routes. Talking about fathers was at the bottom of my list. I flinch a little, then roll to my back as she nestles into the crook of my neck.

"He misses cheeseburgers," I laugh out.

Frankie's amusement shakes her body against me.

"That's deep stuff. You're good at sharing," she teases.

I tuck my chin to meet her gaze, and she's quirking a brow. She's not broken. Only hurt.

"Cheeseburgers are *very* deep, I'll have you know. When you're married to the queen of the grill and perfect seasoning, going months without my mom's special delicacy is a big deal."

She nods, a tiny smile peeking through on her lips.

"Fair point. I'm still a little bitter that you didn't invite me over for meatballs the first night you were home." She holds my gaze hostage with her own wide eyes, and I quickly snap my mouth shut and nod.

"You are right. I owe you an apology. I was still afraid of you at the time, and you had just thrown a Santa suit at me."

She play-slaps at my chest. I capture her hand and bring it to my mouth to kiss.

"You want me to share something real?" I know she does.

She nods faintly.

I run my fingers along the back of her hand, then thread our fingers together. I like the way our hands look together, her olive skin, mine pale and freckled. We would make a beautiful baby. And that thought doesn't scare me like it should.

"Let's see . . . my dad never pushed me to follow in his footsteps. That's something," I say. I've only realized the weight of his parenting as I got older. He never once mentioned the Army as an option for me or pushed me to fantasize about wearing a military uniform or serving as his dad did before him.

"That is something. Your dad is a hero," she says.

I nod and pull her in close.

"He is," I hum, thinking of all the times he's been deployed. He's seen combat, and I'm certain that's why he has never nudged me in that direction. There are things he still has a hard time talking about. But also, his dedication to the job is beyond admirable. He's a true lifer. And now that he's a colonel, he's not facing the same risks overseas as he did when I was a kid. But the risks are always there.

"I really miss him sometimes," I admit. "Even being away at school. I know if he were home, he'd drive down to watch the games."

Frankie lifts her torso, resting her arm on my chest and

propping her chin on her fist. I tuck my chin so I can stare into her perfect eyes.

"I'm sorry," she says.

My mouth slides into a faint smile as I shake my head.

"Don't be. Missing him feels good because it means he's important to me. I'm lucky to love my dad so much and to know he loves me back."

Her eyes blink slowly, and she licks her lips.

"I know what you mean." Her voice is hoarse.

"Hey," I say, sliding down so our faces line up. I hold her forehead to mine as my thumbs stroke her cheeks.

"Your dad is going to be okay."

She nods, her head rolling against mine. Those are just words, but I truly believe them. Anthony said he plans to get tested right after the holiday to see if he's a match, and more of their family and friends will too. I'm willing, and I'm sure Frankie wants to, but if anyone else is a match, I hope she'll let whoever it is step in and keep her from having to go through even more emotionally than she already is.

"Would it maybe help if I told you something I find scary?" My words are out before I really have time to think of them. Maybe it's not the right time. Or perhaps it's the perfect time. Whatever time it is, I've started now.

"Please," she says.

Please. No backing down from that.

I bite my bottom lip and hold her gaze, moving my hand along her face until my thumb reaches her bottom lip, grazing her skin. My eyes go to her mouth, not in a hungry way but a needy one. A possessive one. Adoring one.

"I love . . ." My voice fails, only a stilted breath coming out. I laugh softly, overcome with nerves. I squeeze my eyes shut.

Frankie's soft hands cup my face, her thumbs scratching against the three days of facial hair I've ignored. She seems to like it, so I figure why bother shaving.

"Hey, tell me. Noah, please . . . you can say anything to me. *Anything.*"

Her gaze pours into mine, and my heart is beating so fast I think it might explode. My palms feel sweaty. I should pull them away from her face. But I'm frozen. A little petrified. What if Anthony was right before, that I will fuck up her life.

"I need to hear something good, Noah. Please. Tell me something good. Something . . . *great.*"

My heart skips at the sound of her voice. She knows what I'm trying to say, and she wants to hear it. She wants me. This woman picked me way before I deserved her time or attention. The least I can do is cop to my feelings when she needs to hear the words the most.

"I love you."

I suck in my bottom lip and widen my eyes, holding my breath as I hope like hell she says it back. Her mouth curves up at the corners, the stretch slow, taunting me.

"Show me," she says instead. My insides rush with tingles, but not disappointment because I know she loves me too. She wants the distraction, to feel things that aren't worry.

I roll her to her back and cage her between my arms, dropping my head down until my mouth captures hers. My teeth gently grasp her bottom lip as we kiss, and I coax her head up from my pillow, finally letting go as her hands snake up the front of my shirt.

"I love you." I say the words again. They come easier this time. And I repeat them as her hands still over my heart.

She pulls my shirt up and over my head and I lower myself to her belly, my palm sliding up her thigh and under her nightshirt until her skin is bared to me. I kiss her stomach as she wiggles, arching her back as I slide the fabric up over her breasts. My fingers run over her hard nipples while my other hand slides behind the small of her back, holding her stomach to my mouth.

"Show me more," she hums.

"I love you," I utter against her skin as she pulls her shirt away and tosses it on the floor.

My tongue teases her belly button as I work my way down her body. My fingers wrap around the lacy trim that hugs her hips, pulling her panties down slowly. I kiss just below her belly button, then the trail of hair that leads to her pussy. She lifts her hips, and I slide her panties down her legs before running my palms up the insides of her thighs, spreading her open.

"I love you," I say, my lips peppering soft kisses up her inner thigh.

I pause at her swollen center and let my tongue take its first taste. The slight flick from me makes her curl her toes and arch her back again. I slip my palms under her ass and hold her to my face, humming the words against her clit.

"I love you."

She moans.

My tongue presses against her soft, swollen skin, and I lick slowly, sucking her in, then stroking her with my tongue yet again. She writhes beneath me, her thighs squeezing my head, so I widen her knees, making her take every lick.

"Noah, I . . ." She shivers, and I slide my hand up to push a finger inside of her as I flick her clit with my tongue.

Her hands dive into my hair. She thinks she has to hold me to her, but I never want to leave.

"I love the way you taste. I love this pussy. Fuck, Frankie. I never want to stop eating this pussy," I say, every word I speak marked by my lips against her skin.

I add a second finger, pushing in and out of her as her hips buck against my mouth. Her center pulses, and when her legs close around me again, I know she's on the edge.

"Come for me, baby. You're so fucking beautiful. I love you, I love you, I—"

Her head falls back, and she grabs my pillow to stifle her whimpers, her pussy practically vibrating against my tongue as I flick and tease every last wave of pleasure from her body. When she's finally done, I slide up so I'm lying next to her. Her hand immediately reaches down my stomach and under the band of my sweatpants, but I cup her hand with my own, stopping her while I still have an ounce of self-control.

"Tonight is all about you," I say against her ear.

I shift her until her back is flush against my chest. I can't help that my hard cock is pressing into her ass. And maybe I won't be able to last as long as I hope. But I do want to show her in every way I can how much I mean those words.

"I love you," I murmur into her ear, snaking one hand around her body to cup her breast, teasing the hard peak between my finger and thumb. My other hand slides around her hip and between her legs, my fingers gliding against her still-wet pussy, trembling from her last orgasm.

She gasps, then breathes out, "I love you."

I chuckle softly and press a kiss to the back of her neck.

"You love this," I say, sinking a finger inside of her.

She moans but shakes her head.

"I do love that," she says, squirming in my arms until she's facing me.

She presses a hand to either side of my face, kissing my lips softly before peeling back enough so I'm looking into her eyes.

"I love you more, though. More than any of this. I always have, Noah. I was meant for you."

I shake my head and pinch her chin gently.

"I was meant for *you*," I say, tugging her mouth to mine and kissing her hard.

I let her win our mini wrestling match until her body is caged between my arms. But I don't let her touch me until she comes again, and I make sure this second time takes an hour.

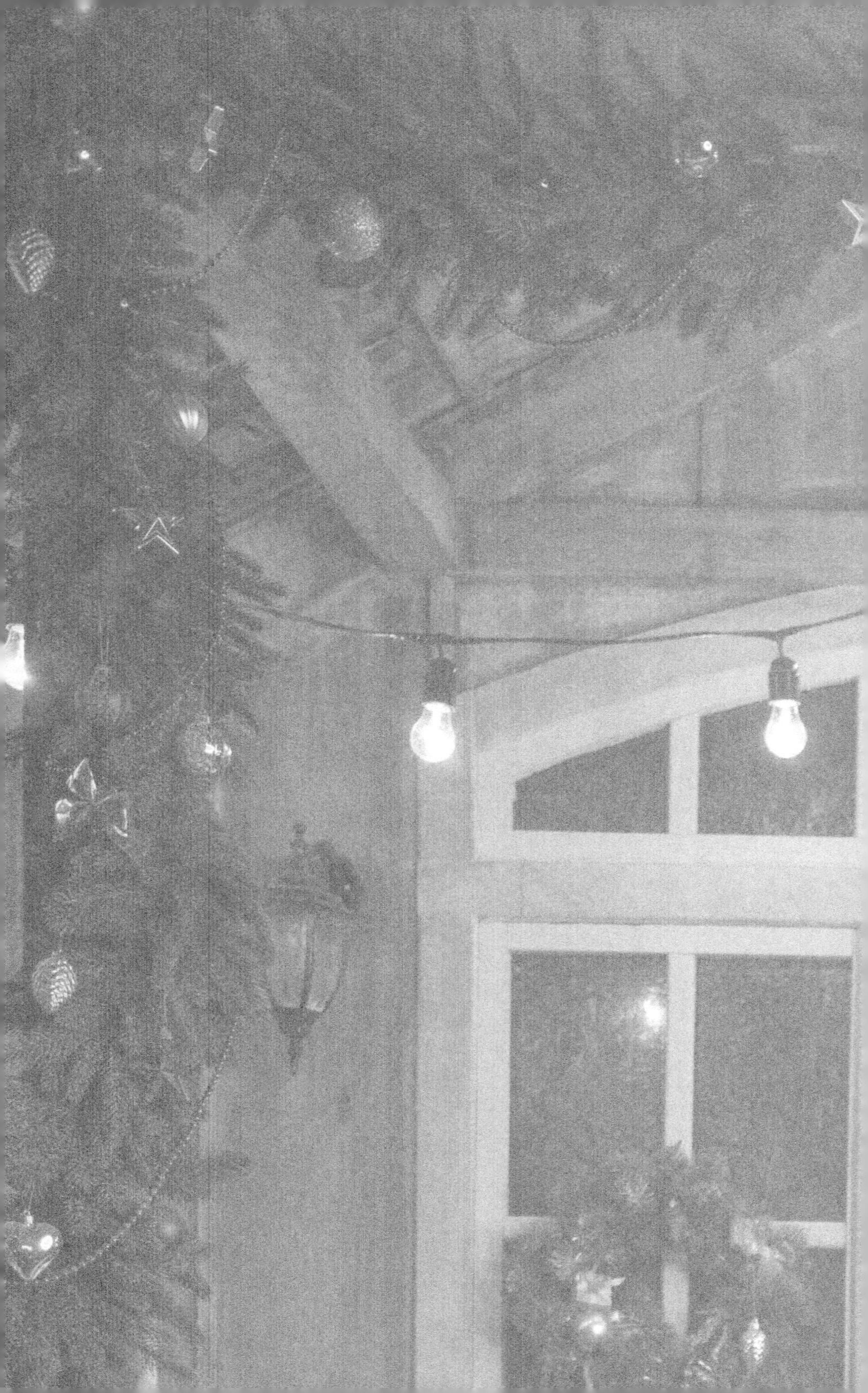

17 / frankie

THE THING IS, my dad doesn't look sick.

I watched him laugh and bellow his trademark *ho, ho, ho* all day yesterday and most of today. The only time I've seen him look fatigued is when he's on the ice. I figured it was just him being out of shape. He hasn't skated much since the boys left for college. But now that I'm looking with clear eyes, I see how tired he is all the time.

He never seems to get enough sleep, even if it's ten hours a night.

I'm less scared now than when I first found out, though. Anthony and I are both scheduled to get tested next week. I think my brother is more worried about the blood draw than anything. For such a rugged, aggressive guy, he's a bit of a wimp when it comes to needles. Not me. I would take the blood myself and walk it in right now if it meant I got the results faster.

"Pretty solid crowd," Noah says over my shoulder.

His hands massage my shoulders, and I do my best to

release the tension and let them fall back in place. Between prepping for tonight's Christmas Eve dinner and finishing up at the photo booth and, well, my dad, I've been a bit stressed.

"It always is." I sigh. I love seeing so many people gather and share a meal together, but I don't love how many of them count on this meal. It's the reason I'm going into community work.

"You did good," he says, circling his arms around me and rocking us side to side. I grasp his arms and admire the room. It's not half bad for a bunch of décor bought from the dollar store.

"You did, too," I say, glancing at the boxes of food stacked on the far side of the room.

"I got you a little something."

I turn to face him with squinted eyes. We agreed we wouldn't exchange gifts because my life is so chaotic and I won't have time to shop.

"I know we had a deal, but it's a simple thing. And I really think you'll love it. At least, I hope you do."

Eying him sideways, I fall in step as he walks backward and leads me to the community center kitchen. The room is thick with the scent of beef broth, roasted turkey, and honey ham. Everything left over is on simmer and warm since my mom and I are the only cooks. I haven't made a plate yet. I like to make sure everyone gets seated and fed first, but damn . . . I'm hungry.

Noah stops at the door to the business office, where I changed for the last time this season into this snug and revealing green dress. At least being inside, I get to wear my furry boots. I know the kids like to see Santa and his helper skate during breaks, and part of the charm of the photo booth is that it's right off the ice. But this year was especially cold. Noah and his damn, accurate snow forecast.

"Close your eyes," he says.

I narrow my eyes but follow his request, folding my hands over my face. Noah's hands land on my shoulders, and he spins me around.

"I'm closing my eyes! Why do I need to turn around?"

"I don't trust you. You were gonna peek," he teases. *I think.*

"I don't like that you don't trust me," I grumble.

"Were you going to peek?"

Was I? Damn it!

"Fine," I huff.

He chuckles, and I hear rustling tissue paper. Such a boy. I bet he stuffed my gift in a bag. He turns me around and pulls one of my hands from my face, hooking a heavy bag on my finger. The red tissue paper still has the purchase sticker on one corner, and the price tag for the bag is hooked along with the gift tag, which is blank.

"It's about what's inside, not the wrapping," he huffs, clearly noticing my scrutiny.

"Yes, true. You're right." I pull the paper away.

My hands touch the familiar stitching immediately.

"Really?" I flash my gaze to Noah as I let the bag fall away, and I hug his high school hoodie to my chest.

"It was always supposed to be yours," he says, taking it from my hands and gathering it up so I can slip my head inside. I may still be Santa's helper, but there's no law that says she can't also be a Noah Drake fan.

I hold the collar up to my nose and breathe in his scent.

"I always wanted this thing," I admit. And by always, I mean since his junior year when the school gave it to him.

"It looks good on you." He smiles, admiring me and sinking his hands in his pockets.

"You look good on me," I reply, twisting in half circles so my skirt sways against my hips. I hug the front of the hoodie to me, and Noah closes the gap between us then tugs on the strings.

"I'm keeping this, just so you know." No way I'm throwing it back this time.

"Good. Because you have a pretty good arm," he teases, tapping his finger on my right bicep.

I smirk and flex my other arm, and Noah's head falls back with a quick laugh.

"That's right. You're a lefty."

I tug him close with my left hand, sliding my palm up his jawline and rising on my toes so I can kiss him. I'm about to deepen it and convince him to follow me into the business office when a throat clearing startles us from the kitchen door. Noah looks over his shoulder as I peer around his body to see my brother standing in the doorway and covering his eyes.

"I'll be glad when the honeymoon phase wears off. I'm getting sick of walking in on . . . stuff."

"Then, maybe you should knock!" I holler. I'm only half kidding.

"Yeah, I know. But there's someone out here asking for Noah. Something about the food donations, and I don't really know the deal, so . . ." Anthony points his thumb over his shoulder, and my stomach tightens because this is happening earlier than I expected. It's Noah's dad.

"I'll be right out," Noah says, turning back to me.

He flinches when our eyes meet, and I realize it's probably because mine are book-owl wide.

"You okay?" he laughs out softly.

"Oh, yeah." I shake my head. "Just, I hate when he walks in on us. That's all."

Anthony is a far better liar than I am, but thankfully, I can kiss away suspicion, which is exactly what I do.

"As long as he doesn't walk in on us later. Because I have things I want to do to you before this outfit goes back in the box for the season." He grabs my ass under my skirt, and I yelp.

"You know, I do *own* it. I can pull it out anytime I want."

"How about when *I* want," he suggests, waggling his brows.

I pat his chest and roll my eyes as I encourage him to follow me to the door.

"My dress, my rules, buddy," I say, pausing with my hand on the kitchen door.

It's quiet on the other side, and I hope Noah doesn't notice the sudden drop in conversation. Before he has a chance to mentally compute it, I crack open the door to meet my brother's gaze. When Anthony nods, I push it open fully and guide Noah into the dining room.

"Where is the pers—"

Noah's words cut off the second his gaze lands on his dad, and without another second passing, he breaks into tears and cups his mouth.

"Damn, did you do this?" He moves toward his father while eyeing me, his smile at war with the tears welling up.

"I'm pretty sure your dad did this," I say. "We were all just decoys."

Noah shakes his head at me, then rushes the rest of his way toward his father, slinging his arms around the man who could be his twin were it not for the graying in his closely trimmed hair. His father falters back a step or two on impact, then pats his son's back with two heavy hands, both tucking their faces in each other's necks and letting the moment swallow them up.

"Thank you for helping with this," Noah's mom says, linking our arms together and looking on as father and son cling to one another amid applause and whistles from their neighbors.

"He really misses him," I tell her.

She runs her fingertip under her eyes, then twists to face me so I can check her mascara. It's a mess. I grimace through my smile and shake my head.

"It doesn't matter. You look beautiful."

She laughs as my mom hands her a tissue. She cleans up some of the black smears, leaving her eyes smoky and red as she steps into her family's embrace, her husband holding both of them close.

While Noah spends some very needed and deserved

time with his parents, I slip into the kitchen and make the three of them and myself a plate. As I'm configuring the plates in my hands, balancing one on my forearm, Anthony slips in through the kitchen door.

"Oh, thank God. Can you take one? I think I'm giving my waitressing skills too much credit."

My brother laughs softly and takes the plate perched on my arm.

"You get food for yourself?" he asks.

"Yeah, I'll take one of these. I wanted to make sure Noah and his parents eat, and I wanted to give them some time alone."

Anthony nods, then picks up a slice of ham from the plate he's holding and takes a bite. "This one's yours now."

"Ha, yeah. I guess it is."

I head toward the door with Anthony behind me, probably still raiding my dinner. Before I push the door open, though, his hand lands on my shoulder. I pause and turn to the side, expecting him to point out something I dropped or to cop to eating my plate clean in seconds. While his expression looks guilty, however, my plate is still full. A new jolt of panic zaps through my body.

"What is it?"

I don't know that I can take one more thing. Not now, at least. I need time to spread things apart. To feel happy about Noah and worried about my dad. And joy for Noah's dad being here. And pride for the holiday dinner.

"No, it's nothing bad. It's . . . it's good, actually."

"Oh." I fall back on my heels and my chest deflates. My pulse needs to catch up now.

"I'm giving Dad a kidney," he says. And just like that, my pulse has no chance in hell.

"What?" I'm pretty sure he doesn't just get to declare such a thing and make it so. We're both getting tested, and so is my uncle. We won't know the results for a few days. Unless—

"Did you already test?"

I can tell by the way his mouth tightens that he did. He lifts a shoulder slightly and blinks through our gaze.

"I had it done right after Thanksgiving. I drove up to Chicago from Tiff, and I told Coach why I needed to miss practice. Noah thought I was taking an early final, and he was honestly so mopey and distracted over you, apparently, that he didn't seem to care when I came home late that night. I wanted to know. Just in case."

My eyes are glued open. I can't seem to blink, I'm so shocked by his news. But also, I understand why he did this. I would have, too, if I knew when he did. I would have needed to do *something*. It's better than feeling helpless.

"I'm a good match, Frankie. I told Mom and Dad I'd already tested after they set up the appointments for me and you. I don't know why I didn't tell you then. I guess I didn't want you to think I was trying to one-up you or something. It's stupid, but I just . . . I need to do this. I'm a good match. Even if you're a match, the doctors said my percentage will likely be the strongest."

"What about hockey? You can't play if you're healing.

And I don't think they let kidney donors play contact sports, so even if you take a year, you . . . you'll be done."

I finally blink when the tears prick the corners of my eyes. Damn these tears. Showing up way too often this year.

"Looks like I'm officially retired from the ice." He shrugs.

"Does Noah know?" I glance over my shoulder to the door where they sit on the other side.

"I'll tell him later. Maybe after his dad leaves. I want him to have a perfect Christmas. And it's not like I'll leave him hanging. I bet Coach will still let me travel with the team. I'd make a great team manager. It's not like I play anyway."

We both chuckle at the hard truth.

"I'm not sure I can let you just do this," I stammer.

He puts my plate down on a nearby counter, then takes the ones balanced in my hands and sets them down as well. Without pause, Anthony pulls me into the tightest hug I've ever gotten from him. His embrace is warm and drowns all my fears with a sudden, odd dose of comfort.

"You don't have a choice, Frankie. I call seniority on this one, okay?"

I suck in my lips and hold in my cry. Damn him for using our sibling rank to his advantage. It's how he always got the front seat or the bigger slice of pizza. I suppose it's only fair that he gets some of the hard stuff, too.

"Okay," I utter into his neck.

And for the first time in days, I think everything really will be.

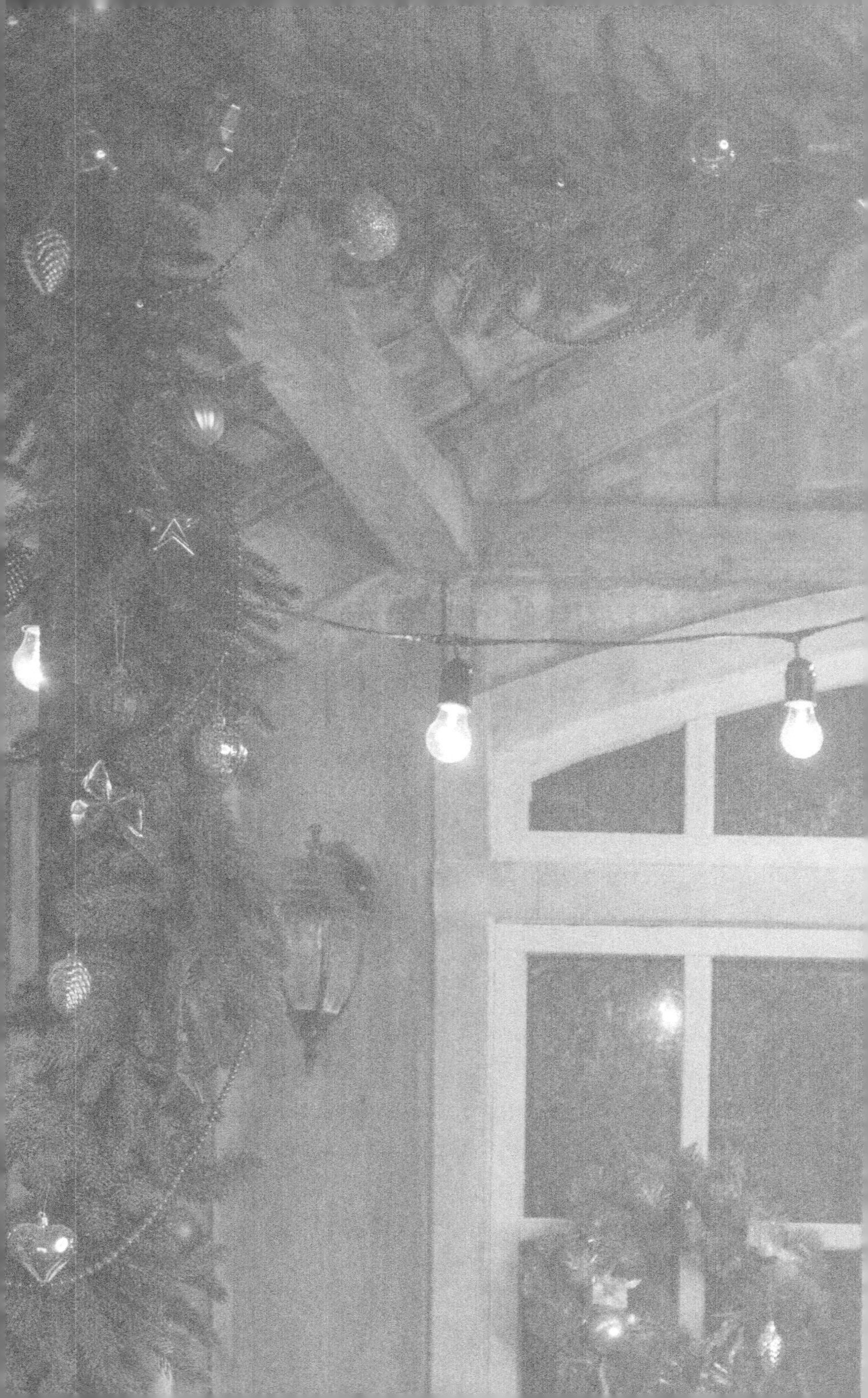

18 / noah

WE DON'T GET A VERY good WiFi signal in the hospital. I feel like an asshole making constant trips outside to join the smokers—*how are there still smokers?* But I haven't missed a single Tiff game and keeping tabs on how they're doing against Western Nebraska without me makes it feel I'm supporting them in some small way.

"Score?" Frankie gets up from her seat when the elevator doors open.

"Still two, nothing," I reply.

She sinks back in her chair, the outline of her body practically imprinted into the leather. I fall into mine and stretch my arm behind her back, assuming the position.

It's surgery day. It's also our first game after the holiday break, and it's against a rival. There was zero chance my head would be in the game, and Coach agreed. Besides, it's a good opportunity for the sophomore, Zach, who will need to fill my skates next season.

"Thank you." Frankie flattens her open palm on my

leg, and I place my hand in hers, just as I've done for the last three hours.

"You keep saying that, but there's no place I would rather be than here."

Her head falls against my shoulder, and I kiss the crown.

"Really? Because I'd rather be in San Diego. Or maybe Hawaii."

We both shake with quiet laughter.

"Anthony's awake," her mom announces, reading a text update from the surgery station on her phone. Frankie leaps to her feet and rushes to her mom's side as she approaches the information desk. I stand and stretch my arms above my head, then crack my neck.

"You shouldn't do that," one of the aides says as she replaces the coffee filter and starts a new drip.

"Stretch? Or shuffle my vertebrae?"

She snarls at me, then shuts the supply cabinet under the refreshment station with a little extra *oomph*.

"She doesn't like me," I whisper at Frankie's side when she returns.

"It's because she knows better, and you don't."

I rub my neck where I stretched it—*cracked it*—and Frankie's gaze follows my hand.

"See?" she says.

"That's not proof of her opinion. I was just giving it more thought."

Frankie's eyes narrow. The last time I cracked my neck in this room, the woman gave me a five-minute lesson on cervical damage and how often is *too* often. She also handed me a pamphlet for anxiety and repetitive behavior, which, okay, that stuff was spot on. I really can't argue with her. I crack my joints constantly out of habit. But I don't think I'm doing any more damage than I am taking bodies into my chest on the ice.

"Come on," Frankie says, snapping me out of my internal debate. "We can go see him."

I shake my head and remember the important part of today. Miracles of modern medicine.

I snag my sweatshirt and Frankie's backpack, slinging it over my shoulder as I take her hand on the opposite side. We follow her mom through the set of doors to the right of the security desk, and a nurse leads us to Anthony's room. He's been out of surgery for a little more than an hour. His dad has a few hours to go.

"Hey, handsome," his mom says, dropping her bag and throw blanket on the chair next to his bed before stepping to his bedside and taking his hand.

"Did they do the nose job, too, then?" Anthony's voice is a little groggy, and his eyes seem to not quite focus on us. His mom glances to me then to Frankie, her mouth in a confused smile.

"Hon, you donated a kidney," she explains.

Anthony rolls his head against the mattress and then meets my gaze, his lips pursed though kind of sloppily and crooked.

"She didn't get it," he says. I replay his words in my head, then laugh.

"Oh, you called him handsome. And we all know he's an ugly motherfucker," I joke.

"Hey," Anthony replies, lifting his free hand to flip me off.

"Careful, you'll lose your IV," I say. He flips me off again, and his mom softly slaps at the hand she's holding.

"I see you're recovering just fine," she says.

"*Mmm*, yeah. They gave me some pain meds, and I hear I might get Jell-O later, so—" He whirls a finger in the air. "How's Dad?" He tries to sit up a little but quickly winces and relents to staying put.

"Probably two more hours. They'll come get me in here," his mom says.

I clear her blanket and bag from the chair and scoot it to Anthony's bedside so she can sit by her son. I poke my head out into the hallway and spot two other chairs, and swallowing my pride, ask my neck-cracking critic if we can borrow them. She agrees when I promise not to crack a single joint for the rest of the day.

The four of us sit in Anthony's room while he dozes in and out. I get a decent signal near his window, so I manage to bring up the stream of the game for the last four minutes. Tiff ends up winning three to one.

It's amazing how quickly an entire day can pass, yet at the same time seem to drag on for eternity. The sun sets while we're in Anthony's room, and the chill of winter fogs the glass. The sun was rising when we arrived to start the day. A celestial event passed in the time it took to move an organ from one body to another.

I haven't done a thing, yet I'm exhausted. I know Frankie is. I tried to get her to sleep in the waiting room, but she was too wound up. The longer we sit with

Anthony, the mumbling of game show reruns spilling from the TV mounted high on his wall, the heavier her eyelids get. Eventually, she succumbs. I cover her with the blanket her mom brought and leave my arm around the back of her chair in case I fall asleep too. I want to feel her wake up.

"Hey," Anthony whispers after a few quiet minutes.

I drop my head forward, and he nods toward his mom, who is passed out in her chair.

"Can you get her a pillow? That's going to kill her neck."

I slip away from Frankie and grab the extra pillow from his bed.

"Apparently, not as much as cracking it will," I mutter.

"Huh?" he says.

"Never mind." I forget he hasn't been awake and with us all day.

I slip the pillow behind his mom's head, and she stirs but falls back to sleep quickly after patting my arm and calling me a sweet boy.

"You always get the credit, don't you?" Anthony grumbles.

I chuckle as I move back to my seat. The room is quiet minus the faint chatter at the nurses' station just outside his door and the steady beep of his monitor. The game shows have shifted to the news.

"Are you sore?" I nod toward his abdomen. He looks down at his hospital gown and shrugs.

"I'm not sure. I think I'm high. There's a lot of tape and shit."

We both laugh, and he winces again.

"Yeah, I'm sore."

I glance to my side to check on Frankie, pulling the cover up her body a little more.

"Thanks for being here," Anthony says. "Not for me, but for her. For them."

His eyes roam from Frankie to his mom.

"Of course. I made a promise."

Our eyes lock for a beat, and his mouth ticks up in a short but accepting smile.

"I'm glad it's you. I mean, I am high as fuck so take it for what it's worth, but if my sister had to fall in love with someone . . . I'm glad it's you."

I nod.

"Thanks." That single word doesn't feel like enough, but the longer we stare at each other, the fewer words are necessary. I knew I found family the day he and his dad asked me to join them for hockey.

"Mrs. Bardot?" A man's voice is accompanied by a soft knock at Anthony's door just before the doctor steps fully inside.

"Mom," Anthony says, rubbing his mom's arm.

"Yes, I'm up. Huh?" She sits up tall and scans the room, jetting to her feet when she focuses on the doctor. Frankie does the same about two seconds behind her mom.

"Please, sit." The doctor's smile is full, and that signals good news. I grasp Frankie's hand as she perches on the edge of her seat. Anthony holds his mom's.

"He's in recovery. Everything went perfectly. And

The Goalie and Santa's Little Helper

barring complications, he should get to go home in three or four days."

"Oh." Anthony's mom breaks down, cupping her mouth as the tears she's been holding in spring loose.

"It's a good day. Or night, as it were," the doctor says, gesturing to the dark window covered in frost.

"Someone will come get you in an hour or two when he's awake." He rests a reassuring hand on her shoulder, and she clasps her hands around his wrist, I think simply needing to hold on for a second. The doctor doesn't seem fazed at all.

"Thank you," I say.

Once Anthony's mom lets go, the doctor moves to the end of the bed and scans the chart.

"I bet you're feeling pretty good right now, huh?" He quirks a brow over his glasses.

Anthony waggles his head, clearly still a bit loopy. Part of that is just his personality, though.

"Well, this stuff wears off. So, take the instructions seriously. You should be back up and running in a couple of weeks. Nothing crazy in the meantime, okay?"

"So, that's a no on hockey?" Anthony says. His mom shoots him a glare, and he holds up a hand.

"I'm kidding," Anthony adds.

The doctor seems to find us amusing, either that or he's gotten really good at playing whatever part the patient needs.

"I need to walk or something," Frankie says, stretching her slender frame in front of me.

"I could use a coffee," her mom says.

"Coming right up," Frankie replies before turning to me. "Wanna join me?"

She holds out her hand, which I quickly accept. We make it to the door before Anthony calls out, "No doing it in maintenance closets!"

Frankie spins around to shoot him a glare, and I hear her mom mutter for him not to be crass in the hospital. But really, what better place? And when Frankie and I pass the maintenance closet on our way to the elevator, we get a good giggle.

By the time the elevator doors close, Frankie drops the mask and lets her exhaustion show.

"We made it," I reassure her, pulling her into my arms as we tick down six floors to the main level.

"I couldn't have done this without you," she insists.

Before the doors open, there's a tiny pause when I think—and maybe hope—the elevator will get stuck. I'm not sure whether it's because I'm exhausted too, or because I feel as though fate is giving me a kick in the ass. But whatever the reason may be, I feel it in my gut. Now is the time. Before those doors open.

"Marry me?"

Her head bops up, and her doe eyes capture mine just as the elevator dings and the doors slide open. Two people step inside with us, maneuvering around us since we've confiscated the very middle. It's uncomfortable and awkward—for them, for us, and for me. Especially for me.

The doors close again, and we begin to head up. I immediately conjure excuses, of ways to take it back and give her an out. And then our companions step out on the fifth floor and the doors close again while we hang in limbo, waiting for someone to call the elevator to them. Wherever they may be. Eventually, we will need to get her mom coffee.

Frankie blinks.

And then she says the greatest word ever formed.

"Yes."

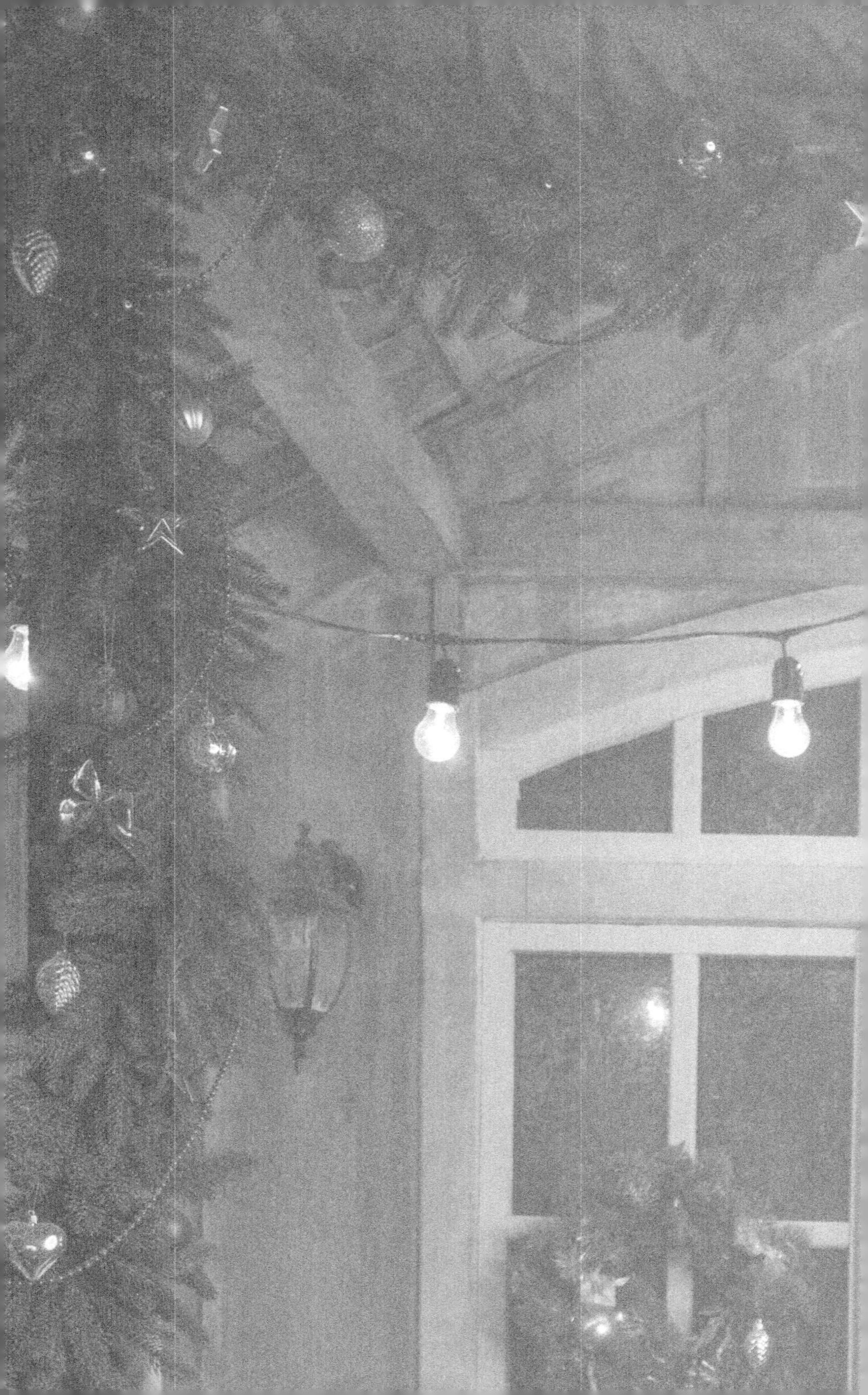

epilogue
One Year Later

frankie

I KEEP CHECKING the parking lot for Noah. He said he would head right from the airport to the photo booth, and I've been explaining that fact to the winter campers who have slapped pucks into my backdrop set at least a dozen times. They think it's funny, and it would be if my head wasn't on the other side of the facade.

"Say eggnog!" Norris dangles a stuffed candy cane above the camera lens to draw the toddler's attention toward him. He snaps a burst of photos in the one second the toddler gives him before squirming his way off my father's lap.

"I hope I got it," Norris laughs out.

"It'll match every other photo we have of him," the mother sighs.

I hand the woman a candy cane and give her an understanding smile. My guy won't sit still for pictures either. Of course, he's twenty-two.

"He's here!" one of the kids shouts from the rink. Dozens of skates peck at the ice as my brother's winter camp squad races toward me. I wave them toward the rink's entrance, but it's no use—they're roaring right at me.

"Sorry about that. I'm glad I made it before they trampled you," Noah says at my shoulder. His arms circle around me before I can startle in surprise, and his lips press cool kisses into the crook of my neck as a gaggle of pre-teen boys and one bad-ass girl encircle us.

"I'm going to kiss him now, so if you find that gross, you should probably go wait over there," I warn, spinning around and leaping into his arms.

He holds my legs around his waist while his mouth covers mine in a deep kiss I've dreamt about for the last month. A few of the boys whistle, and some of them tease us by shouting *gross*. It bounces right off me, though, because I have waited for this kiss. I've been a good girl, and it's the only thing I asked of Santa. The *real* Santa, not my dad.

"Sorry I'm late. I missed you so bad," he says, peppering my lips before setting me back on the ground.

"Do you think we can get the extra hour back from the NHL?" I joke.

"Ha, probably not." Noah grins and holds up his hands, ushering his fans to head toward the table my brother set up to the side of our photo set.

"I'm just glad I beat the snow," he says.

The Goalie and Santa's Little Helper

I glance up at the sky, patches of blue peeking through the cloud cover, and drop my gaze back to him with my usual skeptical squint.

"You sure about that?" I don't know why I question him. He's freakishly accurate about the weather.

He shrugs.

"We'll see." His smug grin tells me he's absolutely sure. Snow is coming. Sooner than we all think.

"I'll sign jerseys and pictures over there, then we'll take the ice for an hour. Hope you guys are ready to work hard!"

He waves the kids into a semblance of a line. They shout *yeah* in unison and follow his directions for the most part, bumping into one another as they battle for the first few spots by the table. Noah has been a Flame for a full month. Instead of spending the year in a smaller market getting games under his belt before heading to the big league, he was pulled up right away, thanks to an injury to Calgary's starting goalie. His saves in his first five games pretty much solidified him as the team's starting goalie for the rest of the season.

Of course, that means he's traveled this year a lot more than we expected. And between my heavy semester in Michigan and his schedule, it's made planning a wedding a bit of a challenge. Maybe that's all right, though, because we sort of blew our families' minds with the announcement. They have no idea he proposed in the elevator the day of my brother and dad's surgeries. They think it happened a month later at Tiff, when we all went to watch a game. We didn't recreate the moment because we felt like it was a rash decision, even if it was. We just wanted our families to feel a part of it. And sure, there was the added benefit of not hearing my brother lecture us on how we're rushing things. Noah and I are simply catching up.

Noah slips into the line waiting to see Santa and signs a few autographs for some of the parents while he waits to see my dad. My father stands from his seat and levels my fiancé with a hefty *ho, ho, ho* when their eyes meet. And when they hug, some of the younger kids in line look on with open mouths, not impressed that Santa knows a famous hockey player, but rather awe-struck that Noah knows *the* Santa, himself.

"You want to give the suit a try, just for old times' sake?" my dad teases.

Noah chuckles and shakes his head.

"I think I've had my fill."

The two chat for a few minutes, then Noah lets my dad get back to work while he heads to the signing table to whip through the stack of photos and the extra jerseys my brother gathered for his ragtag crew.

Since Noah was drafted, my brother spent the summer knocking out college credits and managed to graduate a semester early. We went to his ceremony at Tiff two weeks ago. The hockey team showed up for him, even though he no longer joined them on the ice. He was an assistant coach for the end of Noah's last season, and before graduating, he helped Coach get the team ready and launch their new season. He's decided to use his business degree to start a new youth club with teams for five different age

The Goalie and Santa's Little Helper

groups. He'll split coaching duties with my dad. And now that Noah's dad is officially retired, he plans to help, too.

Mazy shows up to help with the food donations just as Noah and my brother are finishing up with the scrimmage on the ice. My best friend took on handling Noah's pet project this year, and so far, we've doubled the food donations from last Christmas.

"Hey, big guy," my best friend says, giving Noah a welcoming hug as he steps up to help her close one of the boxes filled with cans.

"Thanks for doing this," he says.

My friend blushes from his compliment. This is going to be a lifelong thing, I fear. My best friend will forever have a crush on my husband. It doesn't matter that she has a boyfriend of her own now. And it won't matter even if they get married. Because my guy is Noah fucking Drake, and he's been starring in our slumber party fantasy stories for far too long.

"You sure you don't want to just get hitched this weekend out here? It's a great set?" I follow Noah's gaze to the string of lights that's missing two whole bulbs while a third flickers.

"Yeah, I'm good waiting. I want to do this right. And in summer. On a beach."

We plan to nail down the details over Christmas. While Noah and I haven't had a chance to talk about it much, our mothers have been very busy gathering options and putting together scrapbooks. Since they've been plotting our romance for years anyhow, it only seems right to let them take the wheel on the wedding. My only stipulation is no snow. Oh, and I want to be walked down the aisle by both my dad and Anthony.

They are both thriving a year out from surgery. My brother's recovery was fast. My dad's a little slower, and there were a few worries early on that his body would reject my brother's kidney. But once he turned the corner, his strength came back quickly.

I'll finish my degree this spring, a full year ahead of schedule. It's amazing what one can accomplish when they don't have a boy around to distract them. Though, I don't recommend twenty-one-hour semesters. And I definitely don't endorse piling on school over the summer. My mom worries I've been in too much of a hurry to grow up. But I don't see it that way—not for me, at least. I'm in a hurry to start living.

I flip the sign outside the photo booth to show *Closed for Lunch*, and we all head toward the parking lot and pile into my brother's SUV to head to Noah's for his mom's famous meatballs and pasta. Noah and I volunteer to scrunch together in the very back, even though he is way too big for the flip-down seat. It's been a month since I felt his body close to mine, and I'll take every touch I can get, even the hidden ones in the back seat of my brother's vehicle.

After my brother pulls into the Drake driveway, Noah and I wave him off and promise to be inside after a few minutes alone.

"Do not be gross in my new car," he says, and we both hold up our hands. Noah says, "Goalie's honor," a joke that goes over my brother's head.

"That's what I'm afraid of," Anthony responds, tossing the keys to Noah and instructing him to lock up when we're done.

Once everyone's inside and the front door is shut, Noah pulls me into his lap and kisses me the way I really wanted him to. We keep it PG, but barely. And after this family meal, I definitely plan on heading right to X-rated when I get him alone upstairs. But for now, his raw, rugged kisses, and a hand on my boob are enough.

When my brother opens the front door to the Drake home and peers through his windshield, we pry ourselves apart and slip out of his SUV to join the others.

"You should knock!" I shout at him as Noah tosses back the keys after locking up.

"It's my fucking car!" my brother shouts back, shaking his head before returning inside.

Noah and I laugh, and he turns me to face him, my hands in his, his thumb caressing the platinum band and diamond on my ring finger.

"You sure you want a beach?" he asks, leaning forward and kissing the tip of my nose.

"Yeah, Noah Drake. I love you, and I'll marry you anywhere, but if I get a say, I really want a beach. And sun." I giggle, then pull my brow in and tilt my head.

"Why?" I question.

Noah lifts my chin just as the first flakes begin to fall. I open my mouth to taste them, laughing and smiling when I return to his gaze. Shaking my head, I stretch my palms out and circle slowly in his family driveway to dance in the snow. Then he joins me, resting one hand on my waist while holding my other as he sways us under the quiet hush of the growing flurries.

"You look so beautiful in the snow," he says, brushing my hair to the side and leaning in to kiss my cheek.

And without a word, he takes my ring hand and slips a band on to join the diamond he's already given me. My mouth opens in shock as I look down at my splayed fingers, and he nudges my chin up so I meet his eyes.

"We'll do the big thing in front of everyone else, on a beach. But I kind of like that we got engaged in secret, and I'd like to start calling you my wife, even if it doesn't count legally."

I leap at him and kiss him hard, then rest back on my heels to memorize the way both rings look on my hand. I wish I had one to give him. Before I slip the band back off, tucking it in my pocket, I look up at my husband's eyes, and I say the only thing that matters. Screw the law.

"I do."

THE END

acknowledgments

This will be short and sweet. I wanted this to be a fun escape, and I wanted us to have it this year. So thank you to my own Christmas miracle workers - Brenda, Autumn, my Jersey Shore retreat ladies, Katy, Mom, Tim, Carter and the pack of four-legged friends who let me talk to them this winter.

This book is for you. All of you. If you love it, please tell a friend. Or two. Or seven. And reviews are the best gifts of all.

See you next year!

about the author

Ginger Scott is a *USA Today, Wall Street Journal* and Amazon-bestselling author from Peoria, Arizona. She has also been nominated for the Goodreads Choice and RWA Rita Awards. She is the author of several young and new adult romances, including bestsellers Waiting on the Sidelines, The Hard Count, A Boy Like You, This Is Falling and Wild Reckless.

A sucker for a good romance, Ginger's other passion is sports, and she often blends the two in her stories. When she's not writing, the odds are high that she's somewhere near a baseball diamond, either watching her son swing for the fences or cheering on her favorite baseball team, the Arizona Diamondbacks. Ginger lives in Arizona and is married to her college sweetheart whom she met at ASU (fork 'em, Devils).

FIND GINGER ONLINE: www.littlemisswrite.com

facebook.com/GingerScottAuthor
instagram.com/authorgingerscott
tiktok.com/@authorgingerscott

also by ginger scott

Final Score Series

The Tomboy & The Captain

The Wallflower & The Running Back

The Best Friend & The Short Stop

The Boys of Welles

Loner

Rebel

Habit

The Fuel Series

Shift

Wreck

Burn

The Varsity Series

Varsity Heartbreaker

Varsity Tiebreaker

Varsity Rule breaker

Varsity Captain

The Waiting Series

Waiting on the Sidelines

Going Long

The Hail Mary

The Waiting Series - Next Generation

Home Game

Like Us Duet

A Boy Like You

A Girl Like Me

The Falling Series

This Is Falling

You And Everything After

The Girl I Was Before

In Your Dreams

The Harper Boys

Wild Reckless

Wicked Restless

Standalone Reads

The Moon and Back

Southpaw

Candy Colored Sky

Cowboy Villain Damsel Duel

Drummer Girl

BRED

The Hard Count

Memphis

Hold My Breath

Blindness

How We Deal With Gravity

Printed in Great Britain
by Amazon